QUIET STORM

THE FIRE WITCH CHRONICLES 4

R.A. LINDO

PERIUM PUBLISHING

CONTENTS

AUTHOR'S NOTE

The Fire Witch Chronicles is a spin-off series, following a character from the **Kaira Renn Series.**

There's no need to read the Kaira Renn Series, but please be aware there are some references to the original series.

WELCOME TO A MAGICAL UNIVERSE

Welcome to the secret, magical universe of **The S.P.M.A. (The Society for the Preservation of Magical Artefacts.)**

As my readership grows, it's nice to have a way of staying in regular contact. My **mailing list** is one way. You'll only hear from me when I've got exclusive previews or new releases.

You can also join **my private Facebook group** where all things S.P.M.A. are discussed.

Founders' Quad Map

Society Square Map

BROODING SKIES

The top of The Cendryll's skylight is a comfortable place to be in the current climate, the mood of the magical faculty returning to a familiar quiet. It's been a few days since Taeia Renn gave into his darker impulses, drawn to the pirates of Kelph bursting through the skies on black Williynx: a sign of things to come.

We've learned a lot since our Night Ranging duties were halted: how to fly through the skies on paths of lightning and ropes of fire, the importance of a dead Winter King's visions and the likelihood that battle is around the corner again. I'm calmer than I thought I'd be, sitting alongside my trusted crew, watching the beam of light wash over Society Square.

Sometimes, it's hard to compute how much my life has changed in the last few years — from a sullen, impulsive girl to a Society soldier. The Society for the Preservation of Magical Artefacts is never boring, that's for sure, and it's about to get *a lot more* interesting in the next few days.

The Society elders are locked away in endless meetings, Scribberals used to transport messages to and from The

Orium: the faculty where all laws and critical decisions are made.

Their decisions are bound to involve us: Jacob, Kaira, Conrad, Lucy, Noah and me. Jacob's got his teaching responsibilities but is already committed to defending the sky realms: a shimmering matrix hidden in the stars.

If Kelph is a taste of things to come, it's going to get hairy up there, just like it did when I first stepped beyond the Society Sphere ... across mountainous ranges towards the ashes of Moralev ... before coming face-to-face with a legendary beast.

The difference this time is we've got enemies *and* new magical laws to master: material magic forming the principles of sorcery in the sky realms. It's less about creation than manipulation, something shown to us in glorious form when Thylas Renn drew thunder and lightning from the skies.

As his power faded, Thylas used his gift of blind sight to offer a vision of catastrophe — a troubled heir storming towards the throne he's abandoned with vengeance in his eyes. It's time to make plans of our own while the adults ruminate over what to do next.

Farraday's already made it clear that the heavier burden will fall on younger shoulders this time. We were inexperienced witches and wizards when evil raised its head in the last war, following the rhythms of the adults — adults who put their lives on the line to protect us at every turn, some not making it out of battle.

We'll be leading the charge to the skies, hoping to draw Taeia back from the brink of catastrophe: a mercy mission that's likely to go south when we meet our fallen comrade again.

"We never learnt to read the stars," Jacob comments

from our position on top of The Cendryll's skylight. "Sianna never got around to it."

"We were a bit preoccupied," Noah replies, "learning how to ride lightning on our way to Devreack."

"At least we've learnt a different way to fly," Lucy adds, giving Noah a look.

It's a familiar look linked to her annoyance at Noah's sarcasm — losing its comical power as things get more serious.

"Maybe Sianna doesn't know how to read the stars," I suggest, "or isn't willing to teach us."

"Or it's a matter of discovery," Kaira counters, my friend returning from her sabbatical above ground. "Taeia sat up here night after night, firing out wisps of light towards the stars, getting calmer each time. It sounds to me like he discovered the stars somehow, using the powers within him to uncover the unknown."

"Good to have you back, Kaira," Jacob replies with a smile, the Society tie he grudgingly wears for teaching duties wrapped around his hand. "We'll need your wisdom when we head back up there, assuming you're coming that is."

Kaira nods, sitting alongside me in her regal manner. "I'm ready to meet some new friends," she replies with a smile, turning her attention to the skies and the mysteries hidden within them. "First, we need to find out how to read the stars. Lucy's idea of it working like a Nivrium has got me thinking — maybe my dad and aunt know more than they're letting on."

"They normally do," Jacob replies, running a hand through his long, dark hair. "I doubt they want you to return to battle, Kaira. Maybe that's why Sianna kept her knowledge of the sky realms to herself."

"Maybe the adults are returning to secrecy again," I suggest, glancing at the penchant bracelet on my right wrist, wondering if it will guide us at all in the sky realms. Moving beyond The Society Sphere makes its powers fade, but Thylas Renn explained the relationship between our worlds: how our knowledge can be used to call the elements towards us.

It's a lot easier than it sounds and unless we learn how to read the stars soon, we'll be flying towards danger at a significant disadvantage.

"My dad and aunt live in a different way now," Kaira explains, sending a streak of purple light towards the sky. The Cendryll's beam of light acts like a lighthouse, searching for the stranded on the evening streets. Stranded can mean of lot of things, particularly in light of our current problem with a boy wizard who's found his gifts — stranded between a critical choice which is drawing competing forces towards him.

"They obviously don't want me to fight again," Kaira continues, "but we're long past that now. We're battle scarred after all — all of us in some way — and it looks like we're leading this charge into the skies, so I say we follow Taeia's lead and unlock the mysteries in the skies."

"How?" Noah asks, containing his habit of sarcastic replies.

"With magic," Kaira replies as she fires another streak of light into the evening sky: a warrior girl who's returned to the fold at a critical moment.

THE REST OF US JOIN KAIRA IN OUR STUDY OF THE STARS, sending streaks of light upwards in the hope of discovering something or, at least, *connecting* to something but nothing happens beyond our shower of light fading like fireworks: our moment of fun fizzling out. Whatever Taeia saw or sensed up here isn't being picked up by us — Society warriors not aligned to the sky realms in the way our exiled king is.

"We could sit up here night after night, but I doubt it would tell us anything," Noah comments as we send more streaks of light into the sky ... this time making them stretch as high as possible ... like rockets reaching for the moon. "The irony of it all is that Taeia's ended up being more gifted than we are."

"Marked with different magical abilities," Jacob counters, clearly not happy with the idea of a questionable wizard being superior to us. "We'll only find out if he's more powerful when we meet him again."

"Sounds like life and death," Lucy adds, standing on the top of The Cendryll's skylight.

"Hopefully, no one has to die," I reply, "although a lot depends on how quickly we can locate Taeia's whereabouts."

"In Kelph," Noah adds, standing to join Lucy, the white T-shirt hanging over his chinos.

"A pirate army waiting for our return," Conrad adds alongside me, a strange quiet falling over him.

I wonder if talk of war reminds him of his dad's sacrifice: an incredible act of bravery in The Saralin Sands. Kaira lost her granddad too, maybe explaining why they've both retreated into themselves a little: as if the trauma's resurfacing. We've got more than physical scars but none of us express regret.

There's nothing like the S.P.M.A. I barely think of the above-ground world now, its limited wonders long faded from my memory. Let's face it, after you've stormed through the sky on paths of lightning, whipping out ropes of fire to increase your momentum, there's not much incentive to return above ground.

Our Night Ranging duties will resume at some point, assuming we all survive what's ahead. We can return to the fun of Rebel's Rest then, telling our Society friends all about our adventures in the skies. Conrad edges closer as Jacob releases a flurry of Quij.

Usually asleep once night falls, Quij can be called upon in times of need. Jacob's called them for comfort more than anything else: a brother with a strange connection to Society creatures.

I want to ask him what he saw in the mirror — the one spun into life when Taeia escaped from The Cendryll — but that's for another time. Tonight's about rediscovering old bonds and reflecting on what's passed: a meeting with a fading Winter King and a run in with the leaders of Kelph ... not to mention the Bloodseekers who lined the skies on our return to The Society Sphere ... striking in looks and deadly of spirit.

I can't say I'm looking forward to bumping into them again, although when I do I'll make sure I've got an exit strategy. The S.P.M.A. is a peaceful Society after all, so killing isn't part of the script which isn't to say I'm going to let the Bloodseekers kill *me*. I'll just have to be creative when the time comes.

"I wonder what he saw?" Lucy asks as she keeps her gaze on the stars. "Taeia, I mean."

"Something only a Winter King is attuned to, probably," Jacob responds, holding his hand out for the Quij to rest on. "I was up here every night with him and didn't see or sense anything, even when he started to change. He's found his calling and it's going to be hard to persuade him back from the path he's chosen."

"Mainly because he hates us all," Noah comments, reaching for Lucy's hand who brushes it away. Romance clearly isn't on her mind at the moment, her theory of the sky realms working like a Nivrium on hold for a moment. It makes sense that they might, their changing formation reflecting the temperature of things up there, but the fragile triangle of allegiance isn't presenting itself to us so we're none the wiser.

"Aarav and Casper mentioned the realms surrounding Devreack: Whistluss and Zordeya," Conrad comments, deciding to form a circle of tanzanite light above us. "Casper also said we'd get a call from whoever needed us once Taeia makes his mark."

"Which won't be long," I reply, using the Canvia charm to add some stars within Conrad's circle of light. "If only we could sense what Taeia did ... not being able to puts us at a disadvantage."

"The tables turned, you could say," adds Kaira as she looks down through the skylight, tracking the movements of a familiar figure moving towards The Seating Station on the ground floor.

"Meaning?" Lucy asks.

"Meaning Taeia was always at a disadvantage down here, mainly because of his limited gifts as a wizard. We now know why that was: he was destined for greatness else-where. The question is, how he's going to react to our arrival now the odds are in his favour?"

"It sounds like you already know, Kaira," I say, happy to have my friend back even though it feels different this time.

"I don't but I think Farraday will: the perfect person to answer the question."

"Taeia's hardly going to welcome us with open arms," Noah comments, adding the colours of the rainbow around the circle of light above our heads, "which makes our mercy mission a little tricky."

"Precisely," Kaira replies, "although the real question is where the mercy lies."

"With us obviously," I reply, judging from Kaira's expression it might not be that simple.

"Maybe," she states before adding, "I say we end our star gazing and keep Farraday company. Looks like he's got problems of his own."

"Or the same one," Jacob counters, ushering the Quij towards him before he places them on the glass skylight, their delicate wings fluttering as their colour intensifies. Strings of light stretch out from their bodies moments later, dangling through the skylight. The fine ropes of colour help us make our descent towards a legendary warrior, pondering what lies ahead.

As we slide down onto the ground floor of The Cendryll, I make a secret wish that Farraday can be spared battle this time: the man who's given so much and is so heavily marked by battle.

Mercy is the mission, after all, and who's to say it shouldn't begin at home? To the adults who deserve it most, leaving a group of young warriors to navigate their way to the sky realms once more, on the hunt for a king in exile.

2

A WIZARD'S WISDOM

F arraday stops his pacing at the sight of us, a smile touching his face as we head towards him. He's always been a man of mystery from the days spent above ground, tracking malevs and captors in the night time hours. Farraday's also the first teacher we had, along with Smyck who's sadly no longer with us: another brave soul who gave his life to save Kaira's.

It's an invisible scar that marks Kaira still ... the sense of guilt that she was spared because of a split-second mistake. She never discusses it and doesn't have the look of someone burdened by guilt, but I know my friend well enough to see the cloud hanging over her.

Her dad carries a similar burden although his is more the weight of responsibility, something he wears more lightly these days.

"Star gazing again," Farraday says as he gives Jacob a pat on the shoulder, a greeting between Society teachers.

"Getting ready for take off," I reply with a smile, happy to see an old friend again. There's something comforting about being in the presence of Society legends, particularly when you're about to put your life on the line again.

"Flying without wings this time."

"Isn't that a song?" Noah quips, discovering his comic timing at the right moment.

As Conrad joins Noah, singing their own version of *Flying Without Wings*, Farraday sits on the outer edge of the Seating Station, gesturing for the rest of us to join him.

"You were hoping to find some clues in the stars," he says, producing a vial of Liqin from his waistcoat pocket. "This might help next time."

A glimmer in Lucy's eyes suggests she's onto something. "A remedy to ease hallucinations, seducing the mind into a state of calm."

"That's right, Lucy," Farraday adds, handing the vial of liquid to me. "Liqin has properties to jolt the mind into a trance, making sure venomous energy finds no resting place. As you know, it's mainly used to mitigate the mind-bending screech of the Mantzils, but like all remedies it has other benefits."

"Like bringing the sky realms to life," Kaira suggests, nudging for me to take a sip.

"At least giving you a chance to see them in all their glory."

"So, you've seen them?"

"I've caught a glimpse yes," Farraday replies with a mischievous smile. "It's not somewhere you want to trek to unprepared, so I'd advise taking a sip and heading back up there. Needless to say, Kaira, your dad and aunt aren't ecstatic about your return to the battlefield, so you need to get a glimpse of what's in store."

"And the Liqin will do that?" I query.

With another smile, Farraday produces a handful of

vials, giving us one each. "If you take enough of it. Of course, I didn't suggest this if anyone asks, but the Society elders have a role to play in all this, if only from a distance."

"So, you're going to give this battle a miss?" Kaira asks.

"Like your dad said, Kaira, the adults will be waiting in the wings. Nobody wants a war so we need to practice subtle moves again ... a journey that begins as a mercy mission in the hope stability can be restored.

Also, hold on to the fact that Taeia's never fully embraced darkness, nor has he committed any evil acts. He's troubled and lost — the reason he's ended up in a pirates' embrace — but that doesn't make him a lost cause, at least not yet."

"I agree," Kaira says, getting a strange look from Lucy and me.

Jacob, on the other hand, sits quietly with the vial of Liqin in his right hand. "Taeia's been marginalised all his life, even before entering the S.P.M.A. You mentioned a vision Thylas showed you in Devreack — of Taeia wandering alone above ground, pick pocketing people.

He had no friends then, suggesting he's always been a loner, unable to fit in to wherever he's landed. Imagine what it would feel like knowing you've never been wanted."

My brother looks at me when he says this — the two of us knowing *exactly* what that feels like: a hollow resentment building in you as the world passes you by, sending spiteful glances your way, reinforcing the fact you're an unwanted burden.

Our mum had all the hallmarks of Taeia Renn for a long time, eventually succumbing to the darkness within her. Added to this, I was pretty arrogant in my early days in the S.P.M.A.. The only difference is I found compassion in the form of the Renns: compassion that saved me in more ways than one.

"I know exactly how that feels," I mutter, feeling the buzz of my penchant bracelet, the topaz blue stones glowing softly in the darkness. I imagine the buzzing's a call from my mum sometimes ... the tables turned on a parent who went down the same path Taeia's taking: angry, bitter and thirsty for power.

I'm working on forgiveness where my mum's concerned, so maybe I can extend this to a lost boy with vengeance in his soul. That gets me thinking about what Kaira said earlier — about where mercy lies. She was suggesting it might not be as simple as showing Taeia mercy but, maybe, of his need to discover mercy in himself.

"The reason we're calling it a mercy mission," Farraday adds, echoing my thoughts. "Until Taeia starts a war, peace is our mission as always. Remember, we're dealing with a boy-king with no sense of direction, so don't get hung up on the fact he's fallen under the spell of Kelph."

"Linking up with pirates," Lucy comments, her pixie face showing a touch of disgust.

"Pirates who are skilled at manipulation," counters Farraday, "offering Taeia everything he's always wanted: acceptance and recognition."

"I've still got a bad feeling about things," I state, deciding to gulp down the vial of Liqin, keen to test Farraday's theory of it giving us a vision of the sky realms. "A boy looking for acceptance from a group who only want him for his powers. Imagine what happens when he works that out."

"Fury or glory," Farraday suggests. "We haven't lost Taeia to the darkness yet, meaning his destiny will continue to pull at him until he submits to a single path."

"The seven-year pilgrimage to become The Winter

King," Jacob comments, following my lead and drinking the Liqin.

"If we can gain his trust, we've got a chance," Farraday adds, throwing vials of Liqin to Conrad and Noah. "Drink up lover boys; it might help with the vocal cords."

Deciding not to question our scarred comrade, Conrad and Noah do as instructed.

"It sounds like he was never made to feel welcome here," Kaira comments. "Something my dad feels guilty about now."

"I tried," Jacob counters, a cloud of doubt passing over his face as he says it.

The question of *how hard* we tried is something that dawns on me. Our meetings with Taeia were run-ins where he always came off worse — petty arguments that led to us reminding him of his limited powers.

Then there was his brief time attached to Jacob and The Fateful Eight: a decision made for him by Casper, realising the flaw in ignoring his nephew. Maybe we could have treated him better, but *boy* was he annoying.

"We all tried," Farraday adds as he stands, slapping Conrad and Noah on the back ... a little harder than necessary which gets their full attention. "Now we need to try in a different way. First, by understanding what it feels like to not belong in a place you're destined to excel in: the initial phase of your journey."

"So, we're preparing to *forgive* him?" Noah queries, coughing as he gulps down the Liqin too quickly.

"If Jacob and Guppy can forgive their mother, we can try to forgive those on a similar path," Farraday replies, stepping closer to Noah who bows comically, more out of fear than anything else. "As I've already said, no harm has been done *yet* so it's our mission to minimise collateral damage, starting with understanding what Taeia's resentments will lead to."

"Smashing the things that've made him feel unwanted," Conrad comments as he sits alongside me, offering me a smile: he looks as good as ever.

"Like us," Noah adds.

"We've annoyed him, but we weren't the ones who made him feel left out."

"But we belong to the Society that did," I suggest. "I doubt it makes any difference to him."

"What about the vision of him flying towards Devreack, roaring on the back of a black Williynx?" Lucy questions. "Why would he want to smash the throne that will prove his worth?"

"Maybe because it's linked to him being a Renn," Kaira offers. "The name's been more of a burden than a blessing to him, and it's likely he fears failing in his quest to become The Winter King. After all, he's felt a sense of failure all his life. Why would he want to fail on the path destined for him?

Would *you* be confident of surviving seven brutal winters if you were Taeia?" I pose to the others. "He never grasped magic down here so he's bound to have doubts."

"And being a Winter King leads to a life of isolation," Jacob adds, echoing Kaira's point regarding Taeia's future attack on Devreack. "It's easier to deny your fears than face them."

"Looks like the Liqin's kicked in," Farraday says, lifting his hand in a gesture of goodbye as he heads for the spiral stairway.

"Kicked in?" I ask. "You said it would help us see the sky realms."

"Did I?" he replies with a loud laugh, flicking his hand

towards the skylight ... a charm that releases sprinkles of light over the glass surface. "Keep drinking and wait for the rest."

"That's it?"

"Well, I'd love to have a sing along with Conrad and Noah, but this old man needs his beauty sleep. Remember, we'll be watching from the wings."

"So, we're going back to the sky realms to bond with Taeia?" Noah double checks, struggling to comprehend the idea.

"We'll leave the bonding to you," Conrad comments as he utters 'Comeuppance', taking out another vial of Liqin. "Well, Farraday said to keep drinking."

I shrug and follow Conrad's lead, deciding it beats ruminating over Taeia's state of mind. With bellyfuls of Liqin, we sit together on the edge of The Seating Station, waiting for some mysterious magic to occur.

"The Society stragglers are going to appear soon," Jacob says, "wandering along the upper floors looking for company. We don't want to freak them out; they're fragile enough as it is."

"A bit more time," Kaira urges, an intensity returning to her. Like all Renns, she's gifted with water reading, but she's gifted with something else — unravelling mysteries that seem out of reach. "Farraday wants us to see something so let's hold on."

"*There*," Lucy whispers as the S.P.M.A. logo rises from the marble floor, floating in the air beneath the skylight that continues to glimmer, courtesy of Farraday's touch of magic.

"I say we stand under it," Noah suggests, getting a nod from everyone as the light decorating the skylight drips down onto the spinning S.P.M.A. logo, wrapping it in a film of golden light.

"Maybe we're going to be taken on our own joyride, like
Fillian, Alice and Mae were," Conrad says, remembering
how Taeia's ex Night Ranger crew got a reprieve on The
Hallowed Lawn. They ended up flying through the air on a
glimmering S.P.M.A. logo, zooming off on a tour of The
Society Sphere as a reminder of how lucky they were.

I wonder what'll happen to them on their return, that
thought fading fast when we're in position, standing under
the spinning gold symbol of our endless, magical universe.
The gold light drips onto us all, falling over our hair and
faces, dripping into our eyes. I close my eyes instinctively,
struggling with the heat of the gold liquid.

"Open them, Guppy," Conrad urges. "It's part of the
magic."

Forcing my eyes open, I glance at Conrad who's looking
upwards, his eyes filled with the gold light that runs like
tears down his face. Kaira, Lucy and Jacob are doing the
same while Noah's having the same problem as me, struggling with the pain of the warm liquid.

Pulling him towards me, I say, "Come on ... together. Just
blink when the pain gets too much, but keep your eyes
open."

With a nod from Noah we lean our heads back, letting
more golden light fall into our eyes until we're able to keep
them open ... feeling something pulling behind them as we
rise towards the skylight above ... a touch of magic from
Farraday sending us on.

The Liqin was just the first step ... the shower of light on
The Cendryll's skylight the second, creating a connection
between the earth and the sky. It's a connection we all feel as
we're pulled upwards, our feet resting on top of the spinning
S.P.M.A. logo as we inch closer to the skylight.

I'm reminded of Taeia's dramatic exit a few days ago,

connected by beams of light with his arms crossed, like a messiah entering a state of nirvana. Bliss isn't the word I'd normally associate with our new foe, but the calm feeling washing over me is unlike the mad dash to the skies with Sianna.

Instead, it's more like the feeling I had in the presence of Thylas Renn — the Winter King who offered critical visions in his last moments. As golden light continues to drip down onto us, I wonder where dead kings go, remembering how the skies engulfed Thylas, taking him to his final resting place. It's an unknown heaven I hope I don't end up in too soon.

With a flurry of Quij wakened by the dripping light, we ease through the glass as if it isn't there. None of us speak as we perch on top the skylight again, our faces streaked with gold tears as a pulling sensation remains behind our eyes — a sensation that continues until my penchant starts to vibrate again, softly at first until the topaz-blue gemstones throb with light.

"Lift your penchants to the sky," Jacob instructs, standing as he does so.

No one argues, knowing my brother's mysterious powers with all things magical.

"Lift them up and wait for a connection," he adds.

We follow Jacob's lead, standing in a line on top of a magical faculty hidden from above-ground eyes — Society soldiers about to feel the presence of a universe about to make contact. With our Quivvens glowing beneath our skin, our penchants buzz to life, jewellery of various kinds signalling contact with the skies.

"I feel it," Lucy says, rubbing the penchant ring on the middle finger of her left hand. "It's like a force field running through me."

"The skylight's beginning to vibrate," Noah says. "I say we lift off."

"No, wait," Kaira responds, the purple gemstones in her penchant bracelet glowing brightly in the evening sky. "Jacob's right. We need to wait for a connection; we're guests after all and don't know who to trust."

"What connection are we waiting for?" Conrad asks as the wind blows through his copper-blonde hair.

"A sign of welcome from realms we trust," Jacob replies. "Devreack, Whistluss or Zordeya."

"We're giving Kelph a miss then," Lucy quips, getting used to the idea of flying into danger on a whim.

"Probably a good idea," Jacob replies. "Also, I've got a class to teach in the morning so staying alive is probably advisable."

"That looks like a sign of welcome," I say as arcs of light appear in the sky ... not the lightning we're used to seeing but connected light, falling like branches towards us.

"Wait for the light to connect to your penchant," Jacob says. "Don't move until it does."

"How can you be so sure?" Lucy asks.

"I'm not but just trust me; I sense things sometimes."

"Like when to rescue a comrade from a Williynx attack."

"The same comrade we need to rescue again," Kaira adds, waiting patiently.

"Only this time he doesn't deserve it."

"Peace and preservation, Lucy," Kaira adds. "It's what we live by. Get ready to be lifted into the skies."

With golden tears streaming down our faces and arcs of light surging towards us, I clench my fist in expectation of a shock wave running through me. Instead, I only feel a new sensation in my fingertips, watching as a band of light wraps around my wrist, tightening as it does.

"Well, it feels friendly so far," I say.

"As long as the light doesn't wrap around our necks," Noah adds, looking a little uneasy as strings of light stretch around his right leg. "What if it's Kelph fooling us into a friendly welcome?"

"Our penchants protect us within The Society Sphere," Kaira replies, looking as calm as ever. "Any connection made can only be a harmless one."

"Well, it's getting *tighter*," Noah grunts, hopping on the skylight in a moment of panic. "I don't fancy being suspended upside down again in mid-air."

"Relax, Noah," Conrad says, smiling at the sight of white light forming around his waist. "I've got a belt and you've got a leg brace, that's all. When we're whipped into the sky, just make sure your trousers don't fall down."

The laughter that follows eases the tension until a face appears in the skylight.

"*Bloody hell*," Noah shouts, hopping up and down in shock which causes more laughter.

It's a female face with long, braided hair. Moments later, the skylight shatters beneath our feet, sending fragments whipping upwards, racing towards the stars until they connect with the arcing, white light that frames the sky.

The glass fragments twinkle as they rise until they form a familiar triangle, separated by borders marking known and unknown realms.

"Wow," I mutter, studying the fragments that seem strangely close ... out of reach yet visible as they blink in tandem, bringing the sky realms into view.

It takes us a few moments to realise we're floating, our glass platform now a glimmering map of interconnected realms.

"Now what?" Conrad asks, itching at the scar on his neck impatiently.

"We study the map of glass," Jacob replies.

"Who do you think the face was in the glass?" Lucy asks, walking on air alongside Noah.

"A warrior queen from Zordeya," Kaira replies, deciding to use the Bildin charm to create a seat for herself: a bench long enough for us all to sit on. "Thylas showed me the warrior women in the glass tower in Devreack. He said they'd appear when the sky realms shifted out of sync."

"So Taeia's already made his mark," Conrad comments, sitting alongside me on the bench.

"Looks like it," Kaira replies.

With golden light filling our eyes, we study the twinkling glass fragments together, strangely vivid in the sky.

"Maybe the light in our eyes works like Crilliun," I suggest, "but instead of helping up see in the dark, it works like a telescope, zooming in on distant things."

"Sounds about right," Noah adds. "And the light wrapped around us works like a Nivrium, assessing our intentions."

"So there was no need to panic," Lucy says. "After all, it was only a friendly face sending us a welcome sign."

"Friendly? She looked like a nutter."

"Well, now your *episode's* over, we can concentrate on what the sky's showing us."

"I can only see shapes," Conrad says, pointing to an outline of a familiar fortress guarded by a Williynx. "There's Devreack."

"And there's the sky towers of Kelph," I add, pointing at sky towers in a different part of the triangle of glass.

"Zordeya," Kaira adds, nodding towards the tornados of

light where warrior queens await our arrival. "That's our welcome point."

"So when do we head up there?" Noah asks.

"How about now?" I suggest, uttering 'Smekelin' to release a ball of fire.

No one hesitates — not even Jacob who's scheduled to be teaching in a few hours' time.

"I'm sure the students will appreciate a morning off," he comments, generating his own ball of fire which he blows out ahead of him. "Well, let's not stand on ceremony; a warrior queen is expecting our arrival."

With that, we're off, blowing paths of fire into the air before we storm upwards ... each of us remembering that material magic is the name of the game in the sky realms ... using whatever's at our disposal to navigate, defend and, if necessary, obliterate.

Peace might be the way of the S.P.M.A., but these principles have been abandoned by one of our own: a boy-king preparing to wreak havoc.

3

LIGHTNING & FIRE

The ride to the sky realms is less straightforward than our first journey, maybe because we haven't got a wise guide to lead the way. Whatever it is, it's obvious things aren't going to plan as our paths of fire bend and twist, whipping one way then the other as the first sign of lightning appears.

"Something's wrong," Conrad shouts to my right, struggling to maintain his balance as a blur of movement appears on either side of us. "It's not stable."

"We need to use the Promesiun charm for ropes of light, helping to guide our way," Lucy suggests, whipping out streaks of white light that only make things worse.

"Wait!" Kaira shouts but it's too late, the surge of light pouring from Lucy's hands sending her tumbling through the night sky.

The five of us halt our unsteady flight paths, struggling to direct our lines of protective fire in the direction of Lucy's fall. Her screams pierce the night air as a flash of lightning streaks down ... lightning that seems directed at us.

"We've got company," Kaira comments, deciding not to elaborate but she doesn't need to. Whatever's moving through the air isn't here to help ... Bloodseekers maybe ... or the monsters Thylas warned us of, making me wonder if we're really ready for what's in store.

If we can't make it to sky realms with ease, how are we expected to hold our ground when the enemy strikes? As the sky fills with lightning, Kaira darts out of sight, re-appearing near Lucy's helpless figure, managing to wrap herself in the surge of lightning that fires down towards her.

As she connects Lucy to a strand of lightning, halting her fall, Jacob places his hands together, whispering an incantation that releases a cloud of Quij that burn blood-red.

"A silent army if we need it," he comments as our path-ways of fire begin to fade.

Alternative spells do nothing to remedy our situation, and as rain begins to fall followed by a rumble of thunder, I get the feeling we've entered a training ground: a test to see if we have what it takes to help our comrades in the skies. So far, we're failing miserably so I take matters in my own hands.

Remembering the principle of material magic, I capture a streak of lightning before whipping out the Promesiun charm, forming a connection that charges my body with a blistering force, drawing blood from my mouth and nose. With Noah struggling to capture lightning of his own, I shout a command to him.

"Absorb it, Noah! Connect to the lightning like you did with the suspended rain in Zilom. You have to sense the elements, remember. Let the lightning run through your hands then grab on: touch and timing. It's the same principle up here, but we forgot to connect to the elements before we sped off."

It was the connection Sianna made on our first visit to the sky realms, showing us how to ride on paths of lightning. We added ropes of fire via the Smekelin charm, connecting Society magic to the secrets of the skies. It's a basic mistake but one we're unlikely to make again, each of us connecting to the energy offered from the sky, lightning acting as a stabilising force again.

With Jacob and Kaira taking care of Lucy, Conrad dances through a web of lightning, using the Infernisi charm as a protective barrier against any sudden attacks. It's a clever form of armoury that forms circles of fire around him ... fire that captures the lightning and rain until he's standing knee-deep in water sparking with electricity.

It's a dangerous plan but he hasn't been electrocuted yet, suggesting our penchants and Quivvens are still active, offering a layer of protection. The electricity swarms around Conrad's legs, giving him the fire power he needs should an enemy show its face.

With my boy wizard settled in his battle armour, Noah finally remembers the way he caught the suspended rain in Zilom, using touch and timing to gather a surge of lightning. It's not that different here, except for the courage you need to absorb forces that can shatter you.

The fact our penchants and Quivvens continue to protect us suggests there's some history between the magical worlds — worlds that interact once trust has been gained. A Winter King gave us his blessing, after all, and now it's time to honour his memory by navigating our way out of here.

"Srynx Serum," Kaira says, appearing with Lucy beside us.

We hover over Lucy's shell-shocked figure, applying the healing remedy she comes to her senses. Thankfully, the lacerations on her hands are fresh, meaning the Srynx Serum remedy will heal them quickly. She simply forgot to connect to the elements first: the simple principle of material magic.

Gulping down the remedy, Lucy mutters, "Sorry. It was a stupid mistake."

"Don't worry," Kaira replies. "We're all going to make mistakes; it's how we help each other that matters most."

"You don't think I'm ready."

"I don't think any of us are ready, Lucy," Kaira adds, "but we've never *been* ready; we just manage to find a way."

"And we'll find our way again," I add, echoing Kaira's comments, "so let's get a move on before whatever's moving in the skies turns up to say hello."

"Bloodseekers?" Noah asks.

"Could be," Conrad replies, "but it feels different ... like something inhuman."

"That's comforting."

"If you wanted comfort, you should have stayed in your bedroom," Conrad challenges, a silent anger rising in him. "We told you what war would mean, Noah so less jokes and more focus."

With a sullen look crossing Noah's face, Jacob and Kaira encourage a recovered Lucy to prepare her defences.

"Remember, combined magic from now on," Kaira says. "Nothing singular because it will backfire badly."

"Almost like an insult to the sky realms," Jacob comments as the blur of movement closes in, "using magic not of their making."

"We're guests up here," Lucy comments, rubbing the

orange remedy into her lacerated hands, "meaning we'll have to earn acceptance wherever we go."

"Well, looks like now's the time to earn," Conrad adds.

"Ready when you are," Noah confirms, stung by his friend's criticism.

"Defend together and leave no one behind," Jacob instructs, adopting the role of Society elder although he's the least experienced up here — in a place where the path to safety is as unknown as the venom awaiting us.

THE ENEMY CATCHES US BY SURPRISE ... NOT BLOODSEEKERS or pirates from Kelph but bullet rain that slashes the skin ... firing from every direction until we finally gather our defences and prepare a unified attack. With blood dripping from arms and legs, I manage to release my Vaspyl in time to fend off a renewed attack ... the swarm of bullet rain sinking into my steel shield soaked in ice and fire.

The blood is an obvious problem, pouring from each of us as the storm of bullets bounce off our defences ... brutal rain slamming into our defences until we're forced to adapt our strategy.

"We need to fight in flight!" Conrad calls out, submerged in his cell of fire and water to avoid further injuries.

"Agreed!" I reply, deciding lightning can play a part in this battle dance — the balls of energy captured in my left hand about to be released.

It's the image of Zordeya that gives me the idea, the tornados of lightning still shimmering in a small section of the glittering glass above us.

"Use the lightning as a rocket to blast us up!" I urge, "freezing the bullet rain with the Iscillus charm."

"It could work," Conrad agrees, ducking in the water as a surge of bullets whiz past his head.

"It needs to work otherwise I'll drown in here!"

"Unless the Bloodseekers get you first," Lucy replies, sending a streak of lightning towards familiar faces lining the skies.

"Do you think it's their weapon?" Noah asks, referring to the bullet rain.

"More likely to be competing energy fields blocking our path," Kaira counters. "Zordeya is loyal to the throne of Devreack, meaning the Kelph elite won't want us to make it there."

"Time to teach the bloodthirsty lot a lesson," Jacob says, appearing next to me surrounded by walls of blood.

"Are you hurt?" I ask, shocked to see my brother in this state.

"It's an illusion, Guppy, helping to draw the Blood-seekers in. They've already made their mistake by appearing too soon. We fight in flight, like you said — freezing the rain to stop its momentum — but we make sure the Blood-seekers can see our injuries.

I've used the Magneia charm to form walls of water, letting the blood from my injuries float around me: an impossible temptation for our new enemies."

"Always creative."

"Creative and brilliant," Conrad says, following Jacob's advice as he freezes the blizzard of rain into a vast wall of ice. "Come on, let's move before the ice wall shatters."

With lightning in our grasp and a wall of ice as tempo-rary protection, we blast off again, falling into the rhythm of material magic again. The walls of ice close in on us, clinging to our bodies until we're in our own capsules, spin-ning through the sky as the blizzard of rain intensifies.

I reach for a vial of Quintz, knowing it'll stop the bleeding, but pause when I remember Jacob's second battle strategy: to draw the Bloodseekers in. Thylas described this feral breed as relatively harmless. I'm sure he's right but, then again, he was a Winter King and we're new to sky magic, learning as we go.

Keeping a perfect line of flight, we climb higher, continuing to form new layers of ice as the bullet rain pings off our rocket chambers, weakening in intensity now we've found a way to contain it. The one thing left to do is negotiate a path through the striking figures who line the skies, forming a barrier between the no-man's-land we're in and the twinkling realm of Zordeya.

If it *is* a test, we've survived it so far, relying on our Quivvens to give us some well-needed 'blind sight' as we blast upwards. The brass artefacts maintain their power here, as Thylas said they would, my penchant bracelet also humming as a reminder that Society spells still carry life — as long as we stay attuned to the skies.

I don't know it for certain, but sticking to the Society principles of defence is working in our favour ... rockets of ice to halt a hail of bullets as we blast towards a second enemy: a silent, striking breed flooding the vision my Quivven offers.

With another attack imminent, I check on the others. The beauty of the Quivven is its level of visual detail, like a Follygrin in multi-colour. Thankfully, no-one's losing too much blood, all of us sticking to Jacob's plan of drawing the Bloodseekers in. If they want our blood, they're going to have to come and get it.

They launch their attack like synchronised divers, jumping as one onto our flight path. There's nothing sinister about them as they close in ... or at least that's how it appears until they're on top of our ice rockets. Their finger-nails extend to sharp talons that rip into the ice, a hissing sound coming from them as they work to get inside.

They remind me of the Kyeslin ... the half-human crea-tures that swarmed the Society army when battle raged in far-off realms. There's more control to this breed, though, silent except for the hissing that sounds more-and-more like a chant ... veins bulging in their necks as they dig into the ice.

I keep my eyes closed, relying on my Quivven to illumi-nate the way. No one's ice rocket is under serious threat yet, and we're closing in on the faint tornados marking out Zordeya ... the fragments of glass from The Cendryll acting as a beacon to safety.

A second wave of Bloodseekers poses new problems, the mass of bodies landing on our ice rockets enough to cause cracks in our defences, leaving us only one choice: attack. Jacob's protective shell cracks first, the brother whose idea it was to draw the enemy in.

He's ready with a counter attack no one sees coming ... an army of blood-red Quij flooding into his ice chamber ... Society insects able to navigate any territory and turn violent when needed.

With Jacob's ice shell disintegrating, the Quij swarm out, attacking the bulging necks of the enemy who roar in fury — an incredible roar coming out of a human frame: a reminder that all humanity left them a long time ago.

"Use *ice*," I urge as Jacob appears in a blanket of fire-red Quij ... no other protection except for the lightning he grasps in his hands, and the Quivven to illuminate the way.

It's working, though, the storm of Quij taking the Blood-seekers by surprise — an overwhelmed enemy blinded by the burning attack, some managing to scramble to safety.

There's no safe haven on offer for those who don't vanish in time, though, the loyal Society creatures ripping through skin and flesh until a vampire army is shattered, bloodied and ravaged, leaving us a clear path to a meeting with warrior queens.

4

ZORDEYA

Tornados of light hover in the distance as we enter Zordeya, the realm protecting the sacred throne of Devreack. Safe in the knowledge we're out of danger, Jacob creates a circle of light for the Quij to vanish through: a portal back to the S.P.M.A. now their work is done.

With the thunder and lightning fading, only the rain remains as we hover in the sky, unable to see solid ground to touch down on. As the tornados of light close in, I start to wonder how friendly this new realm is ... no sight of warrior women or anything else.

"Maybe we should do something," Lucy suggests, the lacerations on her hands almost gone now.

"Like what?" Conrad asks.

"Wave, maybe, to assure them we're comrades."

"Waving sounds good to me," Noah echoes, standing on a rectangular stage of light alongside Conrad.

"Falling is what we need to do," Kaira states, crossing her arms before she does just that. "Hovering here suggests we're uncertain — not the statement we want to make."

"Sounds like you've been here before," Jacob adds.

"Thylas sent me to test my loyalty," Kaira explains as she descends slowly. "Trust me, we need to fall until we're welcomed."

"And if we're not?" Lucy prompts.

"We'll end up in the arms of the Bloodseekers."

"I have enough of vampires for one day," I say, stepping off the clouds I've drawn towards me using the Magneia charm.

It doesn't take long for the others to do the same, remembering we're on a mission which, in part, relies on the powers of Zordeya: a silent land of twisting tornados.

ZORDEYA BEGINS TO REVEAL ITSELF AS WE FALL, WARRIOR women appearing from the tornados of light along with waterfalls of liquid gold — waterfalls marking the first visible boundary of a new realm.

As we continue to fall, the women raise their arms, uttering some sort of chant that sends us towards the waterfalls, as if we need to be cleansed of any uncertainty before a formal welcome is given.

This place reminds of Gilweean in some ways — the beautiful land of the Williynx — but there are no spectacular creatures in view and no mass of water hiding a shimmering carpet of colour protecting a sacred axis.

Zordeya is marked with its own beauty and mystery, the liquid-gold waterfalls submerging us on contact. The warm water runs over my body as I sink deeper, confident I'm in safe hands. I rest in the water, imagining I'm floating on the surface of a warm lake.

Jacob decides to use the time to practice his backstroke,

drawing a laugh from Noah who opens his mouth, drinking the water to test something Sianna told us: to let our Quivvens assess anything on offer.

The waterfalls weren't exactly *offered* as a source of nourishment but, nevertheless, the principle's the same: if the water does pose a threat our Quivvens will react. Thankfully, they don't and Noah continues to gulp the water down as if he's swimming in a chocolate fountain.

I glance at Kaira who floats in her waterfall, spurting golden liquid out of her mouth. We've navigated our way without any major mishaps, managing to head off bullet rain and a brush with Bloodseekers, so it's time to have a little fun.

The serious business of tracking down Taeia Renn will come soon enough, but we're still young and there's no Rebel's Rest to give us a break from Society duty. Zordeya's offering that glimmer of joy and it's just the tonic we need, Lucy's laughter a sign she's getting over her mistake on our way here.

OUR MOMENT OF FUN ENDS WHEN THE WATERFALLS DRAIN away, leaving us facing a group of *very* serious soldiers. Aside from the long, braided hair that sparkles with light, their clothing clings to their bodies … clothing made of liquid gold, of course.

It reminds me of the gold that fell from The Cendryll's skylight, dripping down onto us as our contact with a warrior realm began.

"Welcome to Zordeya," comes the voice of a familiar face: the face that appeared in The Cendryll's skylight earlier.

The woman's age is hard to make out, looking ancient one minute then barely thirty the next. Her gold outfit displays a lithe, muscular figure with red symbols on her fingers: a warrior code all the women have.

"You managed to find your way," she adds.

"With a little help from a friend," I reply with a smile, referring to Farraday's guidance earlier.

"Farraday is a legendary warrior," the woman continues. "Adult witches and wizards have a way of looking out for the young."

"That's good news," Lucy comments.

"Necessary lessons will be given," our gilded warrior queen continues, "meaning you'll be shown the way of the sky realms, but not its secrets."

"Can you tell us where to find Taeia?" Conrad asks, studying the swirling pool of water around his feet.

"In time," comes the reply, "but first let us introduce ourselves. I am Mylisia: a distant relative of Thylas Renn. The other women you see here represent a fraction of the force defending Zordeya from threats — one threat you know particularly well."

"Taeia," Jacob whispers, deciding to sink his feet into the pool of water he's hovering over.

I can tell my brother carries some guilt for Taeia's dramatic exit from the S.P.M.A., believing he should have done more to stop him, but we hardly helped in our treatment of him, something I accept now. Obviously, if I'd known he was filled with resentment I would've been more sensitive, but mind reading isn't one of my magical gifts.

I *did* try compassion on The Hallowed Lawn when Taeia agreed to a game of Rucklz. The point of the game was to improve his reaction speed, focusing on his creative ability in counterattacks. He took offence at this, though, firing out a mixed charm that got him into hot water with the Society elders, and a white Williynx in particular.

Jacob came to his rescue then. It was also Jacob who reminded us of how lonely Taeia's life has been until now: the reason he's filled with fury. As far as I'm concerned, my brother did everything he could to reign our lost boy in.

"Yes, Taeia," Mylisia adds. "A Renn who now has the power to release his rage."

"Is he still in Kelph?" Kaira asks, using the water she stands in to wash the blood off her arms.

"Yes," another warrior queen replies, taller than the others and much fiercer looking. "He's taken the throne of Kelph; a mock throne created for his arrival. It's the perfect trick to feed a fragile ego, but one that won't last."

"Why not?" Noah asks.

"Because Kelph can only provide Taeia Renn with hollow validation," continues the woman who calls herself Iyoula. "Worship from a pirate army who will be crushed should they attempt to storm the throne of Devreack. Our boy-king already senses this, fighting the pull of fate as we speak."

"So he *will* return to Devreack," I say.

"Without question," Mylisia states.

"In the way Thylas envisioned it?"

"Storming towards his destiny on a black Williynx ... the moment our sacred realm twists out of time."

"What do we need to do?" Conrad poses, choosing to sit in his pool of water.

We're soaked to the skin already so a little more water's going to make no difference and I'm *starving*, hoping Mylisia can magic up some food. There's always Semphul on hand — the remedy for hunger — but running on a bellyful of remedy probably isn't the best battle plan.

"Learn the ways of warrior queens," Mylisia replies, "beginning with the gift of gold."

THE GIFT OF GOLD COMES IN THE FORM OF THE LIQUID armour our hosts wear ... armour formed from a rare gold falling from the skies ... the same liquid rain that dripped from The Cendryll's skylight earlier. Similar to the way our Vaspyls can morph into any steel object, gold comes in different forms in Zordeya, now appearing in clouds of mist rising through the water we stand in.

I haven't given much thought to what lies beneath our water platforms, sensing that *land* has a different meaning up here. The white fortress of Devreack hangs suspended in the sky, so it makes sense that everything else exists in the mass of space making up the sky realms.

Even the sky towers of Kelph lack floors — or the ones I've seen at least — the reason we created thrones of light when we first visited. It's fascinating and daunting at the same time, knowing you're operating in alien territory with a vengeful heir on the loose.

The gold mist rests on our soaking bodies, covering our skin until a layer of liquid armour forms. I decide to test the armour out, twisting my body into different positions. I'm surprised at how flexible it is, wondering if there's a way of testing it out properly.

Mylisia's made it clear we're going to be given what we need before moving on. I'm happy with magical armour, thankful we've been offered another form of protection before we encounter serious threats. Bullet rain and Blood-seekers were a test, but the pirate army Taeia's fallen in with is likely to be something else.

"As you've realised by now, you have to be at one with the elements. Lightning, fire and ice are already part of your weaponry and now you have the gift of gold."

"Do we have to wear it all the time?" Conrad asks, looking uncomfortable in his shiny outfit.

It makes him look like a ballet dancer although I'm not complaining, running my eyes over his toned body. If only there was a waterfall nearby to wash it off, giving us a little time to reconnect before black Williynx come flying our way.

I still haven't got my head around the puzzle of cursed Society creatures, the beautiful birds originating from the beautiful realm of Gilweean, Conrad's glittering, gold body returning my attention to what's at hand.

"We will show you how gold can protect, guide, heal and attack," Iyoula adds, the fiercer lady studying us more closely. "We will use something similar to a Zombul, generating threats for you to counter. Unlike a Zombul, we hold no silver artefact in our hands so be prepared. Also, keep in mind that all threats in Zordeya are *real*."

"*What*?" Noah queries, wriggling in his gold armour to the hilarity of Lucy. He shares a grimace with Conrad, both boys clearly wanting this over with.

Jacob shrugs his shoulders, taking things in his stride as our assessment begins. This time, no lightning or bullet rain appears but something else entirely: an invisible force field appearing above us, pulling us upwards.

As we use the Magneia charm along with handfuls of water to counter the blast, another problem appears in the shape of winged creatures formed from the sudden rainfall — silent and seemingly harmless until I see the liquid-gold armour melting off me, followed by a burning sensation on my skin.

For the first time since our arrival, we work in perfect unison, each of us uttering 'Promesiun' before we place our arms in the pools of water we stand in. Fully immersed in the power of combined magic, we use our Society skill to send a flood of Zordeya water towards the winged enemy, exploding it into raindrops.

The water creatures reform seconds later, this time storming down on us like kamikaze pilots, our armour bubbling as it sticks to our skin. The burning sensation gets worse, causing Jacob and Kaira to bend double until they activate the Iscillus charm to counter the heat.

Our next move is another synchronised one, forming a bow and arrow from our melting armour. This is no simulation — the pain I'm in reinforcing this reality — and as we fire out a blizzard of golden arrows into the sky, we begin to find our rhythm amongst warrior queens with a taste for violence.

Thankfully, they're on our side, looking on as we take care of the threat before sinking into the pools of water surrounding our feet, keen to cool our blistered skin.

"Your new armour also heals wounds," Iyoula explains, turning to look at Noah who's using the water to dab at his burnt legs. "It's the flecks of gold that are easing your injuries, not the water you're swimming in."

"But it melted," I say, "causing *this pain*."

"The water creatures caused this," Iyoula replies. "Our assessment was to see if you would lose faith in our gift of gold, submitting rather than trusting."

"Submitting?"

"To what was easy, using water as a form of escape."

"So, we've failed the assessment?" Noah queries.

"No, but you've learned the difference between trust and submission."

"But we had no alternative," Conrad challenges, floating in the pool of glittering water.

"There is *always* an alternative," Iyoula replies with contained fury, "and you chose to ignore it. We will try again."

With that, we're pulled out the water, ready to face the water creatures again. This time, I focus on what Iyoula said — the fact we lost faith in our gift of gold.

When it melts and sticks to my skin this time, I stay in position, creating more bows and arrows to halt the storm of heat. It's as if the winged enemy knows our weaknesses, the most intense pain forming around the scars on my arms and legs.

It's only when another blood mark appears that I understand the lesson. None of us jump for the water this time, firing out a counter attack as our armour melts into a single spot on our bodies — where blood marks form again.

Unlike a static shield of protection, we've been blessed with something more unique: an intuitive shield melting to protect our weakest points in critical moments. Another lesson learnt.

"FARRADAY HAS VOUCHED FOR YOU ALL," MYLISIA STATES, studying the Zordeya sky as if another test awaits us. "An endorsement we value highly. However, like your penchants and Quivvens, our gift of gold must be trusted at all times. You now know your armour will melt to protect your blood marks: the points of your body most vulnerable to attack. Interfering with your armour is the fastest way to lose your life.

Beauty and unity carried you in the last war. Protection

and preservation are the principles in this one: the very principles our apprentice king has abandoned. To rescue him from his path of self-destruction, we need to make a connection. You are here because each of you has a connection to Taeia, albeit a slight one, but even the mildest connection could save him."

"How do you mean?" Lucy asks

"With the exception of Jacob and Kaira, you were all Night Rangers with Taeia — the only real sense of family he's ever had. Jacob got to know him through his teaching role, providing him with a father figure he never had. Kaira's father saved him from expulsion or imprisonment in The Velynx.

Despite his deep resentment towards you, each of you have tried to guide him away from the path he's chosen, making you critical to this mercy mission. The briefest moments can mark a person forever. Kaira may not know Taeia directly, but she's returned when it mattered most: a sacrifice which hasn't gone unnoticed.

For Taeia, the S.P.M.A. has a place in his heart if only because it's the home he's never had, symbolised by a level of care and attention he'd never experienced. This will be the anchor he turns to when he realises his only true comrades are the people he despises."

"He's going to ask *us* for help?" Jacob queries, finding this hard to fathom.

"Only when he's truly alone," Mylisia continues, her weave of hair twisting and sparkling as she speaks. "At this point, he will turn to the only people he knows: you He will choose one of you, shifting between desperation and devastation, drawing whoever he chooses into an end game where his fate will be decided."

"Like Russian Roulette," I say, getting a feeling it's going to me he chooses. I'm sure Taeia would love to cast me under his spell, his silent influence dragging me into a game of death.

"Yes," Mylisia replies. "In the end, the real war is within Taeia: two competing forces causing a chasm of confusion in our apprentice king: a chasm many will sink into before this battle is over."

With the possibility of more death and destruction ahead, my attention turns to the blood marks appearing on each of us again — marks shifting position in the way Kaira said they would, moving whenever we enter a different sky realm.

They first appeared during our blood bond with Thylas Renn: a sign of the sacrifices required as we track a boy wizard at odds with his destiny.

5

BLOOD RITES

With a lesson learnt and confirmation that Taeia is holed up in Kelph, I wonder what's next on our agenda. The younger me would have asked for the grand tour, but I've learnt the consequences of impulsiveness the hard way. Noah doesn't have the same reservations, deciding to ask if Kelph has any grand buildings like the white fortress in Devreack.

"The water will take you on," Mylisia replies, ignoring the question.

I glance at the others when the pools of water *don't* take us on, continuing to swirl around our feet in the same gentle way.

"There must be a spell," Conrad suggests, trying 'Entrinias' which doesn't work to no one's surprise. The Entrinias charm unlocks doors in the Society Sphere, but we're a long way from home.

Other charms are tried to no avail, leaving it up to Kaira to show us the way. "Just relax; the water's cooling that's all."

"Where are we going now?" Lucy asks.

"The buildings Noah asked about."

"So, Zordeya's got its own fortress?"

"More a palace than a fortress."

"Not made of gold by any chance?" Noah poses, staring at the water as if sheer willpower's going to grant him access. "Not the friendliest sort, are they?"

"They've handed out some magical armour," Conrad replies, "and healed our blistered skin."

"Blisters they caused."

"Well, actually, the water creatures caused them."

"Sent by the same intense women."

"You're starting to sound ungrateful," I comment, following Kaira's advice to relax.

"I'm just not a fan of gold leotards."

"I think it suits you," Lucy jokes, gesturing for me to join in.

"Never looked better," I echo.

"Any armour that helps save my life is fine by me," Jacob states, tapping his feet in the water.

We return our attention to Kaira who's been here before. Buttoning the blue, velvet jacket, she brushes her back before showing us how it's done.

"Once the water's completely still, just ask," Kaira explains.

"Ask what?" Conrad queries, keen to get on with things.

"To be released."

"That's it?"

"Release me!" Noah shouts, deciding he's had enough of waiting around. It doesn't work though, drawing a laugh from Kaira who's rediscovering her light hearted side — a side I've missed.

"*Set me free*," Conrad adds, joining in with the joke.

As the laughter continues, Kaira places her right hand

over her heart and whispers 'Undilum', vanishing through the pool of water.

"That's it?" Lucy says. "A simple Society spell to undo charms?"

"It makes sense," Jacob replies. "A Society charm mixed with flecks of gold in the water: combined sorcery."

"Well, what are we waiting for?" I add, copying Kaira and vanishing into a tunnel of sparking water. I look out at a world beyond my reach, liquid gold running along every wall and ceiling.

I take in everything around me, my attention drawn to the teenage girls and the creatures accompanying them — some winged with others more human in form.

Unlike the barren realm of Devreack, empty except for a white fortress, Zordeya is richer in colour and life: a palace fit for queens. I smile when the others shimmer into view on either side of me, taking in the wonders of another glittering realm hidden in the stars.

The floors of the palace remind me of The Floating Floor in The Cendryll, offering the illusion of walking on water. This is no illusion by the looks of things ... a sense I'm watching a different kind of waterfall forming a fortress of a different kind.

My second water ride of the day comes to an end at the sight of Mylisia appearing, a brief tornado of light morphing into the elegant figure waving me in. There's no need for spells this time, the tunnel of water throwing me onto a moving mural dominating the floor.

I take Mylisia's hand as I get to my feet, realising my clothes are now dry. It's either the magic of the shimmering gold palace or something else at work, but it doesn't really matter; I'm just happy not to be shivering in soaking wet clothes.

"Take off your shoes," my regal host instructs, studying the mural moving under her feet. It's another wonder of magic, made more interesting when I realise what it is: a map of The Society Sphere with Founders' Quad in the centre.

With my shoes placed on the edge of the mural, I peer at the map of my magical home. I smile when I spot Society Square — The Winter Quarter located in the north. I miss sitting in The Chattering Tap, taking a break from Society duty with Conrad, just happy to watch the world go by.

Thoughts of duty make me question how long I can do this, flying through different realms to maintain peace and civility. As Farraday said, eventually the scars become too much and the burden too great. I wonder when the burden will be too much for me, eventually easing into the shadows of The Cendryll with the legends who've given so much.

"Our worlds have been connected for centuries," Mylisia explains, gesturing to the map.

"The Society elders never mentioned the sky realms until recently," I comment, smiling at the sight of Wimples sweet shop and Merrymopes ice cream parlour — places from a more innocent time.

"Because there was no need," Mylisia replies. "Thylas' demise was sudden, leading to our current dilemma."

"Why don't the worlds communicate more?" I ask, deciding it to be a safe question. "We seem quite separate from what I can tell."

"Each magical universe has its laws and customs, including established boundaries that none cross without permission."

"Almost like different countries."

"Yes, Guppy ... like different countries but sharing the same values and principles."

"Protection and preservation — your version of the Society motto of beauty and unity."

Mylisia smiles, glancing up at the star formation visible through a river of gold. "Indeed."

"Are you born with power to turn into tornados of light?" I ask, feeling a little more relaxed in her company now.

"Yes, Guppy. The warrior women of Zordeya are cast in lightning from an early age."

"*Cast ...?*"

"Connected to a permanent energy field given by the sky: a mystery we nurture and protect."

"How do the girls arrive in Zordeya? Without men, I mean?"

This brings another smile from my imposing host. "Like the boy-king we seek now, not everyone who ends up in the sky realms is born here. In the same way witches and wizards born below discover your world, certain girls realise they belong *elsewhere*."

"A matter of destiny then."

"Destiny and duty: a singular force which cannot be ignored."

"Taeia's doing his best to ignore it."

"With limited success. No heir to Devreack can avoid the seven-year pilgrimage: a fact Taeia senses."

"The reason he wants to destroy the throne."

"Indeed, but this is as futile as joining forces with the pirates of Kelph. In the end, Taeia Renn will be forced to face his destiny: the point at which the sky realms will spin out of time."

"When the war begins."

"A war of sorts, colliding forces without the power to disrupt destiny."

"What's the worst that can happen? If Taeia can't avoid his fate, what sort of damage can he do?"

"He can attack the kingdom he's destined to reign in, stopping time."

"Stopping time?"

"Yes, Guppy. What would have happened if you hadn't faced Erent Koll in the last war? Would your world be recognisable now?"

"No, it would hang in fragments."

"Allowing chaos to reign. Chaos is what Taeia seeks, at least temporarily, forcing the throne of Devreack to retaliate. The moment he tries to jolt a kingdom out of time will be the same moment he sinks into the abyss, using his powers to draw one of you close: the point at which you must act on pure instinct."

"Unless it's an instinct to kill."

"Pity is what you will feel when the time comes, whoever is chosen. It's what you do with this feeling that matters most. Our army will fight by your side until this point, but the final meeting will be a lonely pilgrimage for one of you."

"You're not selling this very well," I say with a smile, deciding the time to stand on ceremony is over.

"I can see why they call you The Fire Witch; a force of spirit burns brightly in you."

"Bright enough to draw Taeia's attention. I've got the feeling I'll be the one he chooses when the time comes."

"You will all share this feeling, Guppy. It's the only vision we can't access, however, suggesting it's either incomplete or not something Taeia's aware of yet. Either way, you have our loyalty until our part in battle is done."

I nod, impressed by the calm she emanates: a warrior queen without fear. Her long, braided hair continues to sparkle, the lightning cast into it turning into tornados of light when enemies appear.

We stop on the edge of the mural as Mylisia clicks her fingers, causing strings of gold to drip from the ceiling — like it did from The Cendryll's skylight — the spell Farraday began to propel us here.

A hand on my shoulder signals the need to stay in position, watching as the strings of gold connect, forming into a wingless bird reaching my waist. The golden creature nods its head towards Mylisia before fixing its eyes on me.

I'm not sure if I should nod back or pat it on the head, my first encounter with a Williynx reminding me of the hidden ferocity contained in some creatures.

"A Deyewinn," Mylisia explains. "A creature with the ability to assess blood rites."

"Blood rites?" I query, holding out my hand as instructed. The creature known as a Deyewinn rests its beak in the palm of my hand, nibbling at the skin. Sensing it would be a mistake to remove my hand, I let the bird nibble away.

"You all have blood marks, appearing first on your visit to Devreack and in the water earlier. Your armour will melt to protect them, but the nature of battle dictates the level of protection possible."

"What can Deyewinn tell from checking blood marks?"

"Whether you're going to live or die," Mylisia replies without a trace of emotion, patting the wingless bird as it lifts its beak, rising towards my face.

The bluntness of the statement surprises me, not because we're discussing death but the timing of the topic. We've just been told to trust our gold armour, and now I'm finding out it's not a guarantee of survival.

That should have been obvious although it still seems

like a contradiction. Sensing it's not the time to bring this up, I let Mylisia explain the Deyewinn's gifts.

"Your blood marks are a sign of future wounds ... wounds your armour will try to protect. Your blond bond with Thylas was a blessing of a sort, mapping your body for potential wounds before they occur.

"So, another type of protection?"

"Precisely, Guppy. Each realm will offer you protection of a different kind. Thylas gave you foresight in the form of a blood ritual; Zordeya and Whistluss will offer you healing properties of different kinds."

"So, the faster we react to seeing a blood mark the better chance we've got?"

"Yes."

"And if we react too late?"

"A healing touch will be on hand."

"From our armour?"

"And other things."

"And the golden bird can tell if any blood marks are fatal?"

Mylisia nods, stroking the Deyewinn who studies the one appearing on my neck.

"And how will that help? To find out if we're going to die?"

"Because death can be averted with forethought."

"By a Deyewinn?"

"No, from rare energy fields found in Whistluss — energy that can embalm the body, drawing out cursed fire. Now, close your eyes."

I remember Casper mentioning Whistluss, probably because he knew Kaira would agree to fight again. The layers of protection we've been given are reassuring, although I can't say the same for the bird staring at me.

Remembering our earlier lesson in trust, I close my eyes and let the wingless bird inspect my neck, nibbling away at the skin which tickles more than anything else. The experience returns my thoughts to Bloodseekers who, I'm sure, would love to be in this position now.

I've got no intention of letting *that* happen, deciding we need to head to Whistluss as soon as we can.

"Well...?" I ask as the Deyewinn lowers its head, shrinking as it does until it melts back into liquid form.

"The blood bond formed with Thylas will serve you well," Mylisia replies.

"So, I'm not going to die?"

"That's unclear but the signs are promising."

"Are the others finding out if they live or die?"

"Some."

"And?"

"War carries casualties, Guppy but remember death can be averted in the moments between life and the hereafter. Our comrades in Whistluss will teach you more. You have the gift of armour and the vision of future wounds. Now, it's time to learn more about our warrior code, something the children will teach you."

I try not to think about what the others have discovered, hoping no one's been told they're going to die. Lucy and Noah are less equipped to deal with such news, stepping into full-blown battle for the first time. It's not something I decide to dwell on for long, turning my attention to more immediate needs. "I don't suppose there's any food on offer?"

"The children are preparing food now," Mylisia replies with a smile: a sign I take as a signal of hope — that we can all survive this war and return to less dangerous adventures in Society Square.

While I'm dwelling on whether I'm going to live or die, my host pulls me towards her, engulfing me in a tornado of light that forms around me, courtesy of her whipping hair. This leads to a new form of flight that propels us through a gold palace, blasting us through room after room until we reach the location where food, friends and new lessons await, from young girls destined to be queens.

6

WARRIOR CODE

The chamber we enter is a different version of liquid gold, a cube rocking from side-to-side as we accept the offer of food from our warriors in training. Like their adult counterparts, the girls have the same braided hair dancing with sparks of lightning.

They also wear the same gold armour as their elders. Their innocent faces and giggles make me wonder how much they've learnt about war, though, but looks can be deceiving: Bloodseekers proof of that.

Everyone's here except Noah who hasn't returned from his meeting with a Deyewinn. Thoughts of death are on my mind after the time spent with Mylisia. Having already survived one war, I'm keen to get out of this one alive, but the wingless bird inspecting my blood mark didn't seem so sure.

Blood marks aren't always clear, I now know, so time will tell how this war plays out. The fact that some of the marks *are* clear is the thing that bothers me the most, unable to shake the thought of losing some of those closest to me. I glance between Conrad and Jacob who both look unaffected by their meeting with a wingless bird.

Kaira also looks calm, leaving only Lucy who glances over at us with a look of unease. Lucy's anxiety and Noah's absence reinforces my fears for them, a growing sense the skies might have already decided who's going to live and die. Magic has a multitude of blessings, though, and I hold on to this as I study the swinging cube of liquid gold. If children can survive a brutal war once, they can navigate a new one in the sky realms.

We were no more skilled than Lucy and Noah when we entered the battlefield, surrounded by a Society army numbering thousands. Curses touched us then but didn't defeat us, scars the marks of our sacrifice. I wear my scars with pride, knowing Lucy and Noah will do the same.

Now, it's just a case of protecting them when thunder rages and pirates appear: two friends who've risked it all to protect what they've come to love. With battle on the horizon, I think of the rare energy in Whistluss; the energy that can avert death.

At least that's something to hold on to — the belief we can survive whatever Kelph throws at us. Hope isn't that far away from denial, though, so the more weapons we have at our disposal the better. As the food is served, I offer my brother a smile, knowing he'll have to return to his teaching role soon.

The Fateful Eight are probably under the tutelage of Farraday in my brother's absence. The idea of absence makes me wonder where Noah is again. If he's reeling from bad news, he'd be better off in familiar company.

On the other hand, I could be over thinking things, imagining my friend staring at a wingless bird melting into the strings of gold as a taste of death hangs in the air. That vision evaporates when Noah fizzes into view, appearing alongside his silent guide.

He's all smiles as he takes his place alongside Lucy, suggesting things have gone better than I thought. I take my food with thanks, smiling at the giggling girl sitting alongside me. Sianna told us our Quivvens would detect the properties of all things offered in the sky realms, so I'm happy to see the rhythmic glow of my Quivven is unchanged.

It suggests I'm not about to be poisoned by the black noodles in my bowl — not the food I had in mind but beggars can't be choosers. The noodles are surprisingly tasty, reminding me of eating tender meat.

It's not a roast dinner but it beats gulping down Semphul: the remedy for hunger that lacks much taste. With Noah settling into things, scoffing anything he can get his hands on, I shuffle up to Jacob to see how his blood ritual went.

"How was your tour?" I ask.

"Dramatic," my brother replies through a mouthful of food.

"Did you meet anyone?"

Jacob nods. "Iyoula. The fierce one who's age changes every time you look at her. I can't work out if she's twenty or eighty-five."

"Somewhere in between, maybe."

"I don't suppose you bumped into a golden bird on your travels?" Jacob asks, judging the answer from my expression. "How did it go?"

I shrug, not wanting to make my brother worry, which is precisely what he does do. He returns his attention to his noodles, a familiar cloud passing over his face. I wonder if telling him will make things better or worse, but decide to anyway.

"It wasn't clear."

"Me neither," Jacob replies with a look of relief. "Let's hope everyone else's was the same. The last thing we want is friends thinking they're going to die."

I stick to silence this time, trying my hardest not to picture who'll fall through the sky, obliterated by an enemy attack we can't contain. The sight of the girls clearing the bowls away is a welcome distraction. Now it's time to learn more about the warrior code of Zordeya, hoping it will help to keep us all alive.

Maybe a Deyewinn can be wrong, wingless birds sensing the future rather than confirming it. I hope so for whoever's been given the devastating news. It's enough to know you're going to be swarmed by pirates and Bloodseekers, the added idea of falling to your death not particularly helpful under the circumstances.

We've got warrior princesses to teach us the battle art of Zordeya, though, giving confidence to whoever's harbouring thoughts of death.

———

THE LESSONS BEGIN WITH A CHORUS OF GIGGLING FROM GIRLS who are already annoying me. If this is part of the training, I'm ready to express my thanks and head onto Whistluss, where we can learn about death-defying magic. The return of the golden bird gets my attention, though, signalling the beginning of lessons with intent.

"The Deyewinn blesses us with luck as well as sensing our fate," explains the youngest girl of the tribe.

"What sort of luck?" I ask, grimacing when another giggle follows.

"The perpetual gift of gold," comes the reply which is sterner this time.

I'm conscious my annoyance is evident, deciding to work on keeping a neutral expression.

"Gold armour you mean?" Jacob asks, giving me a glance I know well; a 'watch your manners' look I take heed of.

"Yes," the girl says, turning her attention towards Jacob. "The gold mist of our realm won't always be on offer, so it has to be created when the enemy nears."

"How?" Conrad poses.

"Like this," the girl replies, bleeding tears of gold that turn into a cloud of dust.

The dust clings to Conrad, morphing into liquid armour quickly. "Cool," my boy wizard says, seeming more at home now in his glittering outfit.

"The gold dust also gives you the power of flight, something you struggled with on your way here," the girl continues, giving her name as Feweina.

I share a glance at the others, recognising there's a lot more to our girl guides than giggling and basic training.

"Sianna offered you powder on your trip to Devreack," Feweina continues. "Powder providing safe passage to a Winter King's fortress. Our gold dust provides you with the dual gift of protection and battle flight."

"Can you show us?" Lucy asks, producing tears to release her own cloud of gold dust.

"First, renew your armour," Feweina replies, "then we can show you the way to our neighbours."

"Whistluss," Noah comments, clearly knowing about the sacred energy that saves lives.

"Yes, the place with secrets of its own; secrets you will need when the enemy shows it face."

"Have you seen Taeia since his arrival?" Kaira asks, shimmering in her gold outfit.

"Once," another warrior queen replies, sharing Kaira's caramel complexion. "He appeared close to our boundaries, accompanied by his pirate army. Remember that Taeia's only affinity is with Devreack — the throne he's chosen to abandon.

Until he aligns himself to his destiny, he will be blind to the powers of the sky realms. The rulers of Kelph will tell him otherwise, suggesting he can reign from afar, but this is simply untrue and likely to be his downfall."

"Did they try to attack you?"

"No, it was more a reconnaissance mission, showing their new leader the way. It will do little to help the boy in question when the time comes."

"It sounds like you'll be fighting alongside us," I add, testing the flexibility of my glittering armour.

"Our first mission to see if we belong here," the caramel-skin girl replies, offering her name as Eaiwin. "The path to becoming a warrior queen is arduous, but we've all made the commitment."

Eaiwin doesn't share the giggling fits of her counter-parts, looking older and wiser as she steps forwards to shake our hands. That doesn't mean I'm underestimating any of the girls in our presence, particularly Feweina whose light hearted manner changes, gesturing to the gold dust swirling in the air.

"You won't always have lightning to guide you," Feweina explains, "so the gift of dust is our second offering. It will be available as long as you remain true to the blood bond made in Devreack."

"What do we have to do to remain true to it?" Jacob asks, running his hands through the dust cloud filling the space.

"Fight to the death if necessary, helping to protect everything that is sacred to us."

"Protecting the white fortress of Devreack at all costs," Noah adds, suddenly looking less at ease ... the memory of a wingless bird enacting a blood rite flooding his mind again, maybe.

"Yes," Feweina replies, "but to do that, first you must learn to turn dust into defence."

"Sounds like it's time for another sky dance," Kaira says with a smile in my direction — an old friend warming to the idea of battle.

"As you wish," Feweina states, turning to her warrior princesses who form a line, grasping a handful of dust as they do. "You are being watched at all times now, so expect to come face-to-face with the boy-king in question."

"Our first taste of war," Lucy whispers, looking hypnotised as the cube of gold begins to swing from side to side.

"Nothing like learning on the job," Noah adds, trying his best to look unconcerned but his nervousness gives him away, a natural reaction before flying into danger.

"Taeia Renn and his army will study us," Eaiwin explains, kneeling with her comrades as she does. "Remember, he knows the ways of the S.P.M.A. and the common defences used. He doesn't yet fully understand the powers of the realms he's destined to inherit, which gives us an advantage."

"Well, let's go easy on him then," I suggest, remembering the need to gain Taeia's trust if we've got any chance of saving him from a tragic end. "Make him realise he's not where he belongs."

"Unless he decides to fire first," Conrad counters, ready to blast into the skies in a flood of gold. "Come on, let's get ready for a showdown."

With two young armies in position, we follow the ritual of our guides who don't spin into tornadoes of light this time, but raise their right arms like Jacob did on top of The Cendryll, humming as they form a connection with the skies.

As our chant grows in volume, I feel my Quivven shift beneath my skin, moving up my arm towards the blood mark on my neck: a sign my first wound is imminent. Whether it comes from Taeia or not is irrelevant now, the skill of turning dust into defence more important. Whistluss can heal critical wounds and our warrior guides are far more than they first seemed: intelligent, fierce and prepared to match enemy fire.

Noah's right — there's nothing like learning on the job so I keep my eyes closed as we blast off, rushing through our cube of liquid gold and into open space once more ... my Quivven offering blind sight and the outline of an awaiting enemy ... led by a boy wizard on a black Williynx ... a bitter smile touching his face.

7

PIRATE ARMY

We fly in unison, the warrior princesses leading the way as we storm through the sky. Clouds of gold accompany us, looking like a swarm of glittering insects offering protection. Protection is already provided by our armour, so we wait to see how dust can be turned into battle flight. It doesn't take long to find out how, Eaiwin taking charge of proceedings.

She's the most intense of the girls, sharing Kaira's gift for leadership, something we're going to need as Taeia orders his pirate army to close in. The swarm of black Williynx glide towards us, no flood of ice released from their mouths but, instead, an unsteady momentum suggesting all's not well in the realm of Kelph.

The sight of cursed Williynx is an uneasy one ... beautiful creatures born in the glittering waters of Gilweean. Whatever spell they're under is fragile, the cruelty of those riding on them evident as the distance closes between us. Taeia punches his black Williynx, reminding me of the way he attacked Oweyna — the white Williynx that almost ripped him to shreds on The Hallowed Lawn.

Our entranced, feathered companions squawk in pain, unable to release their fury on those striking blows onto them, something I'm determined to put a stop to as soon as I'm in range.

"Bloody bastard," Conrad comments alongside me, our clouds of gold dust whipping around us until they settle into a mirror image of each of us, moving our attention away from Taeia's pirate army for a second.

"Look," Lucy says, pointing towards the army of dust surrounding each warrior girl — a replica army of each sky soldier surging towards the enemy. "The gold dust morphs into multiple images of us."

"Helping us to outnumber that idiot up there," Noah adds, looking as angry as I've ever seen him.

The Williynx have given so much in protecting the S.P.M.A., blasting into battle whenever they're called. One of the most unique creatures in our magical world, it's disgusting to see how they're being treated by one of their own, squawking in pain each time another fist lands on their black feathers.

"The gold dust surrounding us will change shape, depending on the level of danger," Kaira explains. "The good news is we don't have to activate the change; the blood bond made with Thylas and our meeting with a golden bird blesses us with the protective forces of Devreack and Zordeya."

"So, we're free to add our own twist on things?" Jacob asks, ready to combine a Society charm with a gift of gold.

"Yep," Kaira replies with a smile, "so let's move our army of dust into range, doing what we can to release our feathered friends."

"Well, one thing's obvious," Conrad says as our warrior

guides prepare to engage, "Taeia's made up his mind where he belongs."

"Maybe," I say, "but destiny's got other plans so let's kick things off with a little introduction."

"What have you got in mind?" Lucy asks.

"Kamikaze flight," I suggest as she utters 'Promesiun', forming a whip of light above her head.

"Crash into battle, you mean?" Noah checks.

"At least make it look that way, drawing Taeia's protection away from him, giving us a chance to release the Williynx before we knock some sense into him."

"Remember, we're on a mercy mission, Guppy," Jacob challenges.

"The sort of mercy Taeia's showing the cursed Williynx, you mean?"

"We can free your feathered comrades," Eaiwin states, appearing within a tornado of light. "This will allow you to isolate Taeia, giving you the chance to bring him to his senses. Be careful not to let your guard down; a single curse will weaken the bonds you've formed here."

With the enemy holding their position above us, circling like vultures studying their prey, I give the signal to surge forwards, turning tears into a band of gold around my feet ... gold that swirls around me until I'm in a tornado of my own, blasting through the air alongside my friends and allies ... a blizzard of light ready to extinguish a dark cloud.

Tornados of light swirl around us all now, the warrior girls of Zordeya directing their force fields towards Taeia's crew. It's an act of unity that does the trick, causing the army of black Williynx to get agitated, their wings expanding as they tilt one way then the other.

The trick of light is used to wash our feathered friends with pure magic, helping to untangle them from the enemy sorcery. It's enough to unnerve a boy-king who shouts at his pirate army to storm forwards, hanging back as they do so in a sign of uncertainty. He's not a king yet — obvious in the way his cowardice reappears at a critical moment: a glimmer of hope that he can still be saved from himself.

With the pirate army closing in, I release my first blast of attack, blowing gold dust onto my Promesiun charm before I whip it upwards, aiming for the neck of the nearest enemy. The bald-headed figure takes the bait, diverting his black Williynx away from the attack and straight into a wall of trouble ... trouble in the form of a swirling army that smothers the cretin from Kelph.

Completely blindsided by the attack, Taeia's desperate comrade blows his own magical force field into action ... a circle of grey smoke that forms a noose around his Williynx's neck ... an action he expects us to counter.

"Wait for our signal," Eaiwin orders from somewhere in the distance. She's still part of the blizzard of light disrupting Taeia's plans, but she sounds as if she's right next to me: another wonder of warrior queens. "We will free the Williynx and extinguish this vagabond crew. Taeia Renn is your responsibility ... keep him engaged long enough to make him question the path he's chosen."

As the Williynx falls through the sky, struggling for breath, I reply, "We can do that," leaving rescue to our young guides ... a unified army surrounding a boy who would be king.

With Taeia's pirate crew abandoning him, quickly over-whelmed by our combined force, the Williynx host new companions, gliding calmly through the troubled skies calmed by their rescue part. The majestic creatures hover below us, still disoriented by a curse unravelling under a layer of gold.

Soon, Taeia's going to have more than a few old friends to worry about, and no one's going to save him from a Williynx's fury this time. He's got other problems to deal with first, though, facing ex-comrades armed with blessings from winter kings and warrior queens.

"Have you come to arrest me?" Taeia shouts out sarcastically, perched on the only Williynx still under his silent influence. "Or maybe you've come to kill me."

"Still letting others do your dirty work?" I counter, abandoning any ideas of kindness. "A coward too scared to be king."

A blast of fury smashes into our shimmering army, rebounding as it does before it's caught by Taeia, smiling arrogantly to remind us of his new powers.

"I can hold the sky in my palm, but you need a borrowed army to protect you."

"At least our army sticks around," Conrad counters, sending a cloud of fire Taeia's way.

When he swallows the attack, a realisation dawns that he's far more than a lost boy; he's got *frightening* powers ... powers he's keen to use on *us* ... probably the reason he's hung around, pretending to be helpless without guidance from a dark corner of the sky realms.

"Well, *arrest* me!" he shouts with a wild laugh. "The Night Rangers of the S.P.M.A. coming to the rescue!" Another blast of fury thunders towards us, splintering the army of dust this time ... dust that rushes towards our boy-king until warrior princesses intervene. They send out a battle cry to the Williynx who've shaken off their hypnotised state. Ice blasts surges towards a shocked Taeia who vanishes out of sight, re-appearing at a distance.

With the Williynx free of their cursed chains, they return to their full glory, glistening with colour as they shape-shift to avoid his attacks. A circular shield of ice dominates the sky line, spinning as it closes in on Taeia. The Williynx collects us as they spin out of danger: a unified army of soldiers ready to keep darkness at bay.

The circular shield of ice splinters and reforms, adapting to each mode of attack as it reads every sinister move ... moves that are becoming predictable as Conrad directs our path ... the boy born to fly.

"We separate and splinter him," Conrad says as our Williynx shape shift again, spinning into reduced forms as the sky turns on Taeia: a Zordeya sky aligned to a dead Winter King.

"No fatal wounds," Jacob counters. "Whatever he's done, we've got clear instructions to save him, if we can."

"Splinter his skin and puncture his confidence," Conrad explains. "We've got back up on the way; Mylisia's leading a charge from inside the gold palace. We move Taeia towards her crew, making sure we don't do any real harm."

"He definitely *can't* hold the sky in his palm," Jacob adds, echoing Conrad's point. "See how the lightning's shattering his spells. He's powerful but not in the ways he thinks, weakening when he threatens the fragile balance up here."

"Let's keep him occupied until he's cornered," Kaira suggests, capturing a bolt of lightning that surges past. "Lightning and fire to send him reeling, then we can free the last Williynx."

"Not much of a mercy mission, is it?" Noah asks, ducking to avoid snakes of fire.

"We've got our orders," Lucy replies as our Williynx army tilt to the right, adjusting their position underneath Taeia's erratic figure, sensing how exposed he is now. "Let's get it done."

With Mylisia's army of warrior women in position, we

pivot upwards on our feathered companions, their bodies expanding to an enormous size, creating a wall of feathers Taeia flies into. I'm not sure what to expect next but Conrad doesn't wait, launching himself into the air ... directly into the flight path of a comrade who's betrayed everything we hold sacred.

There's no time to second guess Conrad's move, knowing we have to fight as one so I jump with him, spinning in the cloud of gold dust that moves wherever I go. The wall of Williynx feathers frames our battle ground, Kaira, Jacob, Lucy and Noah jumping in unison as the lightning crashes down, surging through us to add additional blessings.

It's the first time I've felt the full force of the sky realms, my body rippling with power that I send in Taeia's direction ... an electric force field that sears his skin as it whizzes past him in all directions ... Society soldiers and warrior women surrounding a boy crippled with resentment.

We stick to Conrad's plan of splintering skin and shattering confidence, doing enough to rock him off his black Williynx who's drawn to Mylisia's army, looking as though they're offering the lightning to us. It makes sense since we're nowhere near controlling the elements up here.

Elements critical to our plan of out containing Taeia as his attacks become more erratic. Driven by bitter emotion, he aims his fury at different people until the Williynx close in, roaring in fury as their enemy tries to make his exit. The warrior women have got other ideas though, using the lightning to form a web around Taeia, entangling him in a magical force field destined to be under his command soon.

Well, destiny's going to have to wait because we've got our target where we want him — marked by minor injuries that will heal quickly. What isn't going to heal so fast is the damage he's done to legendary Society creatures, and the failed attack on a realm laced with gold.

Mercy is still on my mind as the Williynx respond to Jacob's call, my brother vanishing into an ice tunnel that offers protection from the final assault. The sky battle is won for now, leaving the warrior queens of Zordeya to decide how compassion can be found in a boy so bent on revenge.

8

BATTLE CRY

With Taeia's power muted in a web of wonder beyond his control, the combined army of Society soldiers and Zordeya women stand on a pathway of light, framing our hollow king. I look between Mylisia and Iyoula, wondering which one is going to take charge.

It doesn't take long to work out none of them are, their attention turning to the two girls who guided us in our cube of gold earlier: Feweina and Eaiwin. They said this battle was the first test of whether they belong in Zordeya, a heavy burden falling on their young shoulders as their hair spins above them — ready to rip a tornado of energy through Taeia should he make any false moves.

It doesn't look like he's going anywhere at the moment, writhing in the web of lightning that charges through him: a reminder of the sacred powers he's turned his back on. It's not over yet, though, the sky too silent as Taeia relaxes, studying the sky as if he's waiting for a winged carriage to arrive.

Nothing would be a surprise at the moment, checking

my gold armour's still in place as lightning fills my hands, something I hope I don't have to use. Capturing an enemy is one thing, but convincing them to abandon their strategy is something else entirely.

As Feweina and Eaiwin blow a handful of gold dust in Taeia's direction, the rescue mission begins its first phase ... a tentative move towards the lost boy by the two girls ... hair sparkling with lightning as if they sense a counter attack. We're going to find out if rescue is possible now, a familiar smirk returning to Taeia's face as the glittering dust wraps itself around the web of lightning, lessening the force field of energy charging through his body.

With the line of Williynx observing behind a sheet of ice, probably to stop them ripping Taeia's head off, the warrior princesses work as one, gliding towards our target as their hair continues to spin, ready to form a tornado of consequence should this touch of compassion backfire.

The first rumble in the sky suggests it might do just that, Taeia laughing as the girls close in, our unified army holding their positions.

"He's up to something," Jacob whispers in my direction. "Look at the way he's studying the sky, as if he expects back up to appear."

"Maybe it's just his arrogance," I suggest, remembering that laugh in the hidden section of Pat's Caff, where Night Rangers meet before their evening missions begin.

"It's more than that," Conrad says, squeezing the ball of lightning in his hand. "He's going to blast the girls out of existence; I can feel it."

"Let's not make any sudden moves," Noah suggests, blowing a mouthful of gold dust over his Vaspyl ... glittering, morphing steel ready to shield or strike.

"Jacob's right," Kaira states, gesturing towards the

Zordeya elders, gliding closer to their young apprentices. "It's a trap and there's definitely something shifting in the skies."

"Pirates ... got to be," Lucy says, looking down at the arc of light acting as our stage.

"Well, get ready for another sky dance," I add, deciding on whips of fire and lightning.

Taeia's got formidable powers now, after all, meaning any missteps are going to be punished, returning me to thoughts of mercy. I mean, how much mercy can you show an unrepentant wizard?

The sky dance begins with streaks of light lining the sky, similar to the ones appearing on our first visit to Kelph. It's the same vision as before ... two lines of soldiers riding pathways of light ... tightrope walkers of a different kind. Taeia laughs again at the sight of his rescue party, crossing his arms and legs within the web of lightning as if he's at home: a sight that makes me wonder if he's trapped at all.

The hundred-strong rescue party aren't coming to welcome us to their pirate kingdom this time, obvious in the way they splinter into smaller factions, scattering across the sky until we're surrounded ... a move that releases the might of warrior women and Williynx ... spinning in tornados of light and carousels of colour as the battle begins.

Bullet rain and Bloodseekers were our first taste of the enemy, but the shuddering sky signals something more sinister: a faction of Taeia's comrades rushing towards his webbed cage. Mylisia and her female army are there in a flash, forming a combined tornado of light that wipes the smile off Taeia's face ... a force field that shimmers and stretches until it flies towards the enemy, a phenomenal force sending part of his rescue party flying.

As Taeia looks on calmly, still trapped in his web of

lightning, the Williynx signal their return to battle with a streak of ice spiralling through the air. They shape-shift to avoid the mouthful of venom released by each pirate whizzing around them — the time for Society soldiers to make their presence felt.

"We split up," I suggest. "Half of us contain Taeia's rescue party; the others keep an eye on Taeia. He's playing a game with the girls which is going to end badly."

"I'll keep an eye on Taeia," Jacob offers.

"Me too," Conrad and Kaira say in unison, leaving the rest of us to add to Zordeya's defences, ready to put our learning to the test.

We're washed in liquid-gold armour, our penchants and Quivvens glowing as we enter the fray— Society sorcery helping to ignite the magic hidden in the skies.

"Use gold dust more than lightning," I suggest as a blast of venom surges towards us, blown by the rescue party who deactivate their lines of light, camouflaging themselves in the skies as they do. "They expect a one-dimensional attack, ready for us to reach for the same thing every time.

Use the gift of gold instead, trusting our armour like we were told to. Then add Society magic to blast the pirates out of sight."

Lucy and Noah nod as we spin out of harm's way. With the enemy darting in and out of view, I prepare to join forces with Lucy and Noah, checking on the others who wait for Taeia's move. He's going to make a move alright, glaring at his ex-comrades with contempt. I don't see this mercy mission working out for him.

"Call the Williynx," I say as I dodge another blast of venom, the magical dust coating the Infernisi charm — rings of fire working as an effective shield. "We need feathers for our next move."

"Why's that?" Noah queries, sending a wave of fire towards the enemy, blistering the skin of the pirate crew attacking from all angles.

With Lucy adding her own slice of sorcery, firing out discs of morphing steel, I reply, "Our own disappearing act."

"When do we call them?" Lucy asks.

"Now!" I reply, whistling to the yellow Williynx who releases a shower of feathers I rush towards. Deactivating the rings of fire, I continue to spin as the feathers cover my body, uttering 'Verum Veras' as they do.

The invisibility charm works a treat, the feathers becoming a shimmering curtain of red and gold. With Lucy and Noah following suit, we form the counter move I hoped for, hovering out of sight as the surviving pirate army search for us in the shuddering skies.

"Thank God that worked," Noah whispers as we glide towards each other, remembering sound still carries in our protective curtain.

"Material magic," I reply with a smile, uneasy at the sight of Taeia looking our way, as if *he* can see us just fine. It feels like a stand-off now, between the remaining pirate army waiting for his command and the trio of forces surrounding him.

"Why don't they retreat?" Lucy whispers, pointing to the disoriented few hanging in the sky, bodies broken by her spinning discs of metal, multiplying to shatter skin and bone.

"Silent influence," Noah replies, referring to the way Taeia put The Fateful Eight into a trance, before making a dramatic exit from The Cendryll.

"What sort of king lets his own kind suffer?"

"They're not his own kind, Lucy," I reply, "and I think he likes to see others suffer."

"And we're supposed to be saving him?" Noah comments with a touch of bitterness.

"The reason why he's playing with us," I add, "sensing we're not authorised to harm him."

"So, we just let him go?"

"With a message," I add. "Come on, time to find out what game Taeia's playing."

With a battered army hanging above us, we float towards Conrad, Jacob and Kaira who stand with the guardians of Zordeya — silence returning as the skies settle again. I fight against my better instincts, deciding not to hold Taeia's gaze. If I do, we'll probably return to our verbal sparring matches until one of us reacts.

"The Fire Witch in places she doesn't belong."

I decide to ignore the comment, forming circles of fire with my finger to signal disinterest.

"Aren't you going to say anything funny?" Taeia prompts, glaring at me as he does. "It's a perfect opportunity. I'm trapped and you've smashed half of my army."

"They're not really your army, are they?"

"They are now; I'm their king."

"Nope," Jacob chips in. "You're a wizard on the run, currently hanging in a web."

"Well, I didn't have the best teacher," Taeia counters with a smirk.

"Fair enough," Jacob replies to my surprise. "We didn't teach you well enough or earlier enough, so what now?"

"I get out of this and say my goodbyes."

"Which means we'll meet again," Kaira adds, studying a relative she barely knows. "Fate has a way of calling the Renns, Taeia. Trust me, I know."

"Well, it isn't calling me."

"It's calling you now," Kaira counters. "The reason why

you haven't tried to attack us. Your destiny is in another realm, guarded by a Williynx of another colour: the colour that will mark you as The Winter King."

"And you're all here to *show me the way*," Taeia adds with a bitter laugh. "Make me realise what I'm missing out on. I've made my choice ... to have nothing to do with *kings*, *destiny* and *orders*. I'd rather be a pirate king than any king you recognise. I *belong* in Kelph and that's where I'm staying."

"Unfortunately, it isn't that simple," Mylisia says, deciding it's time to end the stand-off. "Visions suggest you pose a threat to our universe — the universe you've been called to."

"And if I do pose a threat?"

"No mercy will be shown."

"More pity from the privileged," Taeia replies before whispering something to his remaining rescue party — words that trigger them into action, crawling onto the web of lightning on his command.

We look on as his loyal followers shudder on contact with the web, absorbing the lighting containing their king. Like the broken bodies hanging in the sky, Taeia's silent influence is at work again — secret sorcery turning battle-hardened sky soldiers into mindless zombies. Whatever magic's at work, it's clearly working because the web starts to shrink.

"What now?" Conrad asks, ready with some sorcery of his own.

"We blind them with gold," Eaiwin replies, the warrior girl with a point to prove.

Turning to the other apprentices, she produces the shower of gold dust required, stamping her feet to begin a chant. The Williynx respond to the chant, gliding in a circle above us as Taeia emerges from his cage of light. As the chant increases in volume, we work as one, preparing a blinding blizzard of gold.

Taeia's prepared for this though, turning the web of lightning into tentacles that stretch out towards us. He might not hold the sky in his palm but he *is* connected to its force in some way, firing the tentacles at us. With the Williynx darting in and out of the lightning firing out from Taeia's body, our apprentice king increases the ferocity of his attack.

The power and speed of enemy fire knocks Eaiwin off her feet, the young girl spiralling upwards, looking helpless as she floats towards the lifeless pirate army who snap into life. A blizzard of ice comes to her rescue, courtesy of the Williynx who've rediscovered their powers ... coloured feathers glistening as they freeze the enemy ... a strange vision of ice graves floating in the sky.

The rhythm of war begins as Taeia *swallows* lightning, turning his head to the sky to absorb its powers. His eyes turn white as the force field floods his body ... a blistering mass of energy pouring from his mouth and hands as a blizzard of gold closes in on him.

The chant of the Zordeya army continues followed by a new phase of attack — the weaved hair of each warrior woman loosening as it stretches out in the sky, looking like an enormous spider about to gather its prey.

Bullet rain appears again but this is easily dealt with, ice shields protecting us as our pirate king shouts in fury, trying to bend the sky to his will as swords of fire rain are added to his arsenal: another futile attack thwarted by a wave of water, courtesy of the Levenan charm.

We have golden armour allowing us to activate Society charms, and Taeia only has his limited connection to the sky realms — not enough to defeat a unified army even if he *can* swallow lightning.

He's a boy out of time, attacking the people he should be protecting, cutting through the glittering blizzard surrounding him as his splintered comrades float in ice graves: a sign his power is fading. Escape is the only thing on his mind now as he searches for a way out, raising his arms to gather more offerings from the skies.

It's not *his* world yet, something he realises when weaves of hair stretch towards the thunder Taeia calls ... thunder that surges down like tornados towards an apprentice king in retreat.

It doesn't reach him in time, though, the warrior women of Zordeya proving what *a true* connection to the sky realms means: a *complete* affinity with the elements that shift away from Taeia, connecting to the weaves of hair that stretch out at an impossible distance.

We're here to learn as much as defend, watching the stunning display of power ... thunder falling under the influence of the Zordeya army, chanting as they stamp their feet again.

The women and girls jerk their heads one way then the other, turning the thunder on Taeia and the ice graves decorating the sky ... the reason for the dual attack obvious as blood pours from the suspended dead, causing the stage of battle to shift again as Bloodseekers close in.

With Taeia outgunned and his dead army dripping with blood, a familiar uncertainty crosses his face — the uncertainty of a boy-king doubting his powers. He isn't truly connected to the skies, only the lightning absorbed and released at will.

Nothing else is under his command, proven by the way the thunder rejected his call. He's going to have to accept his fate or die in denial. I'm all for compassion, but a wizard who hates what he is, turning that hatred onto others, isn't likely to find any.

"Vaspyls for the Bloodseekers," I suggest.

"Agreed," Kaira replies, uttering 'Comeuppance' to retrieve her ball of morphing steel ... steel that's sent the way of the vampire army feeding on the dead.

The new enemy adjusts quickly, biting into the dead before dodging the multiplying threat, some more successful than others. It's what they do next that throws us off guard, spitting out strings of blood that they grab onto. They fly towards us as they swipe out with their extending nails, catching me on the neck as I focus on moving Lucy out of harm's way.

The speed of their flight is difficult to adjust to, mainly because they jump from one blood strand to another — a problem the Williynx sense as they fly towards us, creating a protective wall of ice.

"Guppy, you're bleeding *a lot*," Jacob comments as he checks my neck.

"Shame we're not in Whistluss," I joke, remembering how my blood mark appeared before we left our gold cell. "I could do with some death-defying remedy now."

"You're not dead yet," Conrad adds with a look of concern, comforted by the sight of the vampire army blasted into pieces by the Williynx's fury.

"We need to get you back," Kaira says, moving along the wall of ice to check my condition. "The Bloodseekers' nails are tainted with venom."

"Great," I reply with a forced smile.

"It's my fault again," Lucy adds. "I didn't react in time."

"We fight as one, Lucy," I offer in a sign of reassurance.

"But I shouldn't need defending all the time."

"You'll save me plenty of times, trust me; it's the way of war."

"Well, this one's coming to an end," Noah states, gesturing through our wall of ice towards a retreating Taeia ... stranded and alone as a warrior chant fills the Zordeya sky: a chant of victory as a battered boy is blasted out of sight.

9

HEALING TOUCH

We return to the liquid-gold palace in one piece, the blood pouring from my neck being the immediate concern. Conrad, Jacob and Kaira look particularly worried. Luckily, we've got a remedy for stopping the flow of blood - Quintz - although I'm not sure it's designed to deal with injuries sustained in other realms.

Our gold armour fades once we touch down, the room we're now in formed of interconnected mirrors. It's a strange sight to behold when you're losing a lot of blood, endless reflections of yourself that fade from view.

"The mirrors assess the extent of your injuries," Mylisia explains, looking as regal as ever as she steps towards me. "We can only treat it once we know this."

"So it's bad?" Jacob asks, taking another look at my neck injury.

"It was expected," Mylisia replies. "Remember, your blood marks signal the point of attack: an inescapable part of this particular battle. Each of you will sustain your own injuries over time; it's merely a matter of where and when."

"Sounds like we need to be in Whistluss," Kaira

comments, remembering the sacred energy used to embalm the dead and dying.

Considering my injury doesn't feel critical, I doubt I'm dying but my vision is beginning to blur. Whatever the mirrors are looking for, I secretly wish they'd speed up the process, feeling a little awkward as blood drips over my all-black outfit: not so much a Ninja warrior but a blood-soaked girl with a lot to learn about the sky realms.

"Whistluss can wait," Iyoula counters, shaking out her long hair as if thunder's still surging through it. "We have our own healing mechanisms for such injuries; it just requires a little patience."

"She's losing too much blood!" Conrad shouts suddenly, realising his mistake when the warrior queens circle him.

"Raised voices have no place here," Iyoula adds with a strange degree of calm. "Respect the magical force field we now stand in, and learn ..."

When the mirrors begin to move, shifting like a pack of cards, the learning begins — a flock of blue and gold birds appearing in each one as if we're staring through windows of time.

"The Jacqus and Deyewinn," Noah whispers, slightly awe-struck by the sight.

We all met a Deyewinn earlier today, the golden bird that assessed our blood marks. The Jacqus is mainly found in Senreiya: the beautiful realm of earth towers resting beneath a multi-coloured sky.

Like the Williynx, the blue birds protect a part of The Devenant — the source of all magic in the S.P.M.A. — but there must be more secrets contained in their wings.

"Time to step through," Mylisia states, gesturing towards the mirror that moves towards me from the maze of glass.

I'm used to magical portals so I follow our guide's

advice, stepping through another layer of liquid glass into an awaiting flock of magical creatures.

―――――

WE'RE BACK TO OUR WATERFALL SURROUNDINGS, BUT NOT THE place we were in earlier. This time we're standing at the bottom of a stone chamber, looking at the winged wonders decorating the space: Williynx, Jacqus and golden Deyewinn.

"They can fly?" Noah asks, staring up at the Deyewinn who soar towards the open sky, dripping with gold as they do.

"All birds can fly, Noah," Mylisia replies.

"Even birds without wings?"

"Magic has its benefits."

It certainly does and I find out just *how much* of a benefit a Deyewinn can be when the gold drips onto me, falling onto my wound until the bleeding stops.

"Our golden companion offers blessings beyond assessments of blood marks," Mylisia explains, looking in my direction.

"So, it can heal all wounds?" Conrad asks.

"Only the magic of Whistluss can do that, but Bloodseekers present no fatal threat to the living."

"So our own remedy would have worked?" Lucy prompts.

"To stop the bleeding, yes; to remove the venom, no."

"How do you feel now, Guppy?" Eaiwin asks, the giggling girl I first met in a swinging cube of gold.

"Like something's running through me."

"The Deyewinn's healing touch, neutralising the Bloodseekers' venom."

"That's good to know. Where would the mirrors have taken us if my injury was critical?"

"Elsewhere," Iyoula replies mysteriously — a reminder some secrets aren't going to be revealed to us. "Now we move on to the next phase of your visit. You all know about a Jacqus' particular gifts."

"I don't," Noah pipes up, putting his hand up as if he's in a lesson.

"Remember Sianna telling us about the Jacqus?" Lucy says. "How they'll come to our rescue at critical moments."

"Sort of."

"Well, what else do you need to know?"

"I don't know ... maybe what their magical powers are. The Williynx can shape-shift, breathe ice and release magical feathers to unlock things. The Jacqus sent out some weird energy field that made Guppy's nose bleed; I remember that in Sianna's place in The Royisin Heights, although I doubt that's going to save us."

"Which is what you're here to learn."

"Great!" Noah replies with a smile, putting his hand up again. "So, we're going to ride the blue and golden birds?"

"In a way," Eaiwin replies with a familiar smile: a sign another lesson is about to begin.

"As you already know, the Jacqus creates a crushing force field of light," Mylisia explains, suggesting I step into one of the waterfalls to wash off the remaining blood. I'm not keen on getting soaked again but, then again, having blood-stained clothes isn't the best thing when travelling up here. Bloodseekers have given me my first battle scar, so washing off the scent they react to can only be a good thing.

"And that's their main protective element?" Jacob asks, watching as one of the blue birds in question touches down, its small form resting by his feet.

"Yes," Mylisia adds. "Protection and destruction at once. The force field can crush bones and shatter wills — enough of a threat to halt most enemies in their tracks."

"Most?" Conrad queries.

"Those with common sense."

"Not Taeia then," Lucy adds.

"Our boy-king is within touching distance of his full powers and he knows it," Iyoula adds as the warrior girls decide to take flight, propelling themselves upwards with their spinning weaves of hair ... towards the golden birds who take them higher still.

The girls stand on wings of liquid gold — two girls on each Deyewinn — proudly perched on a battle platform formed of liquid magic.

"*Brilliant*," Conrad whispers, itching to be carried into the skies on his own Deyewinn.

"It sounds like he's determined to run from his destiny," Kaira says.

"Which is the reason for a change of strategy," Mylisia adds.

"Which is?"

"Tracking Taeia down in his own territory."

"*Kelph*?" Noah queries. "We'd be walking into a trap."

"Not with what you will learn in Whistluss. It's the only way to prove your intent: mercy not malice."

"And if he *is* waiting to kill us?"

"He isn't," Kaira replies, watching as the warrior princesses soar through the Zordeya sky, yelling in delight as their golden companions rise higher, painting the sky with streaks of gold.

"You don't know that," Lucy challenges.

"No, I don't ... but how long before his pirate army realises he isn't an all-powerful king? He's returning to Kelph injured, having to explain the ice graves floating in the sky. How many more dead bodies will it take before the Kelph elite turn on him?"

"Not long at all," Mylisia replies, echoing Kaira's point. "Which is when you will be needed: at the point when humility is forced upon our hollow king. He will need a way out of Kelph, and those that guide him need to be trusted faces."

"It makes sense," Jacob states, placing his hand onto the Jacqus near his feet, causing the blue bird to create an energy field around his legs. "Battling Taeia isn't going to get us anywhere. We need to go to him as outsiders in his world, knowing what it feels like to be at the mercy of others."

"The real mercy mission," I utter, coming to terms with a dangerous endgame.

"Indeed," Mylisia agrees. "Until we find mercy in Taeia, our fragile allegiance remains at risk. His death must be avoided at all costs: a catastrophic outcome for us all."

"Because only the skies call time on a Winter King," Conrad says, remembering what Sianna taught us on our visit to Devreack.

"And the skies will punish us all should we fail."

With the image of an angry sky turning against us, I step out of the waterfall and look up at the golden birds gliding through the sky. They carry their companions on wings formed from strings of gold, looking like they're also preparing to enter a land of pirates.

"HOW'S THE WOUND?" JACOB ASKS IN A MOMENT OF PEACE, only the Jacqus keeping us company now.

With our young hosts having fun in the sky, and Mylisia's crew leaving us to ponder the consequences of failure, we perch on the stones in the centre of the circular chamber, watching the waterfalls' quiet rhythms.

"All healed up," I reply, touching my neck.

"Well, at least your blood mark didn't kill you?" Noah offers in his usual attempt at comedy, the look on his face reinforcing what I feared — that his meeting with a Deyewinn didn't end with good news.

Mylisia said that some of us wouldn't be so lucky with our blood marks, referring to the lifeline waiting for us in Whistluss. Also, our blood marks move when we move to a different realm, meaning there are more wounds waiting for me.

"Do you think we'll get a ride on those golden birds before we leave?" Conrad asks, clearly missing his days as a sky rider.

"Maybe if we ask nicely," Lucy replies, "although these blue birds seem more interested in us."

"Not another crushing hello," Noah quips, jumping when a Jacqus flutters in front of his face.

"Relax, Noah," Kaira advises. "They're just being friendly."

"They drew blood last time we met."

"Stop being a drama queen," I add. "Sianna was teaching us their protictive powers, and only because Conrad got a little overprotective."

"A gentleman always protects his fair lady," Conrad comments, saluting like a lieutenant.

"I prefer Fire Witch to fair lady."

"Just doing my duty as your boyfriend."

"By turning a Jacqus on me?" I tease, watching as the birds circle around our feet, inspecting us a little more.

"It looks like they're about to turn on us again," Noah adds, grimacing at the sight of a flutter of blue feathers.

"Stand still unless you want to offend them again," Kaira advises, offering me a mischievous smile.

"You're up to something," I say, getting a laugh from my friend.

"Who me?" Kaira replies, finally able to throw off the cloud of the last war. "I'm just here to help out."

"Okay, so what are the birds up to?" Noah asks, leaning back as the blue birds inspect his cardigan and long, dark hair.

"They're deciding if they should send us on," Kaira explains.

"To where?"

"To the place with life-saving energy."

"Whistluss?"

"Yep."

"Can't the Williynx take us there?" Jacob asks.

"Mylisia thinks we should let the Jacqus and Deyewinn take us there."

"By blasting us into the sky?" Noah queries, taking a deep breath at the thought of this.

"Something like that," Kaira adds with another laugh.

"You're joking?" Noah comments, but Kaira isn't joking by the look of things ... the old mischief returning as a flood of blue blinds us.

"*Bloody hell,*" Noah says, flailing in the wave of blue light buzzing around us. "I can feel a nose bleed coming on."

"Maybe keep your eyes closed for this part," Kaira adds, squealing in delight as we're spun upwards, our bodies submerged in the wave of light that guides us on.

As we rise higher, the waterfalls lift with us, reaching up to form a pathway of water as we climb towards the sky. The laughter of the Zordeya girls fills my ears until I get my balance, managing to stand on my pathway of water that stretches across the sky.

"Yes!" Lucy shouts, following the morphing waterfall as it leads us on, to another realm hidden in the sky.

ELEGANT TRAVEL

The waterfall continues to stretch across the Zordeya sky. Gold is the accompanying colour as we make our journey to Whistluss, the magical realm that's going to come in handy if any of us sustain fatal wounds.

Whatever life-saving energy it's got, I can't wait to experience it, thinking I should try it out on my non-fatal wound — more of a scratch laced with Bloodseekers' venom.

I'm sure the vampiric lot have more tricks up their sleeve, making our education in Whistluss even more important. The question of how we get there is left to Kaira who lets out another laugh: an old friend who's rediscovering her warrior ways.

As the paths of water rise, they rotate to bring us closer together ... Kaira and Conrad on either side of me now with Jacob sending a salute to Lucy and Noah.

"It feels like I'm walking on water," Noah comments as the warrior girls glide above us on their golden companions.

"That's because you are, you idiot," Lucy replies with a familiar roll of the eyes.

Her pixie look will give her an advantage when we head into Kelph, tracking down Taeia before it's too late. To the untrained eye, Lucy looks harmless: small, lithe and pretty with the skills to match. Something tells me she's going to be a secret weapon when we meet Taeia again — another magician who was an outsider not long ago, struggling with bouts of insecurity in the face of grand wizardry.

As our pathways of water climb higher, I study my reflection in the water and see something else ... as if I'm looking into my own personal Nivrium ... a water reader showing me my future. There's going to be a war, all right, with all the major players involved, but there's no sign of our boy-king in the flickering image of battle, making me wonder if fate has already marked his card.

I study the image as the water wraps itself around me, closing in on me to allow a closer look at what's ahead: a personal journey through the moving towers of Kelph as the enemy closes in.

From the look of things, the pirate army is preparing for our arrival, keen to make sure they protect their prized asset. If my water reading is right, we'll all have our own paths to follow in pursuit of peace — a pilgrimage to prove our worth before the endgame begins, towards a king out of time in a realm devoid of loyalty.

As the water becomes more volatile, the vision of my future fades, returning my attention to the others spinning in their own streams, probably coming to terms with what's been offered to them, courtesy of another form of magical travel.

Thoughts of what lie ahead will need to wait, though, as the water falls away from us, forming beneath our feet as we surge upwards, using the Magneia charm to keep our balance.

"Maybe we just keep going until we fall off," Noah says.

"Or get attacked by more bullet rain," Conrad replies with a smile.

"A good chance to test out our new skills," Lucy adds, clearly wanting to rectify her mistakes on our journey so far.

"Well, I'm missing the Bloodseekers," Jacob jokes, deciding to do a handstand as we surge upwards, drawing a laugh from us all. "Things look different from down here," my brother adds as the water splashes his face.

"I think you need to get back to teaching," Kaira comments, deciding to go one better with a single-hand handstand.

"I'm having too much fun."

"Not missing your students?" I ask, joining in by resting on my belly.

"I'm sure Farraday's keeping them entertained."

"Or terrified," Noah adds as he grabs onto the tube of water, pretending to be terrified.

With no enemies in sight, we take a moment to relax, remembering to hold on to humour and wonder wherever possible. The Deyewinn fly closer to end our water games, followed by a call to jump on from our girl guides. Increasingly comfortable in our new surroundings, I time my jump well, landing on the wings of the golden bird alongside a familiar face.

"You will need an introduction," Eaiwin explains as our golden companions glide through the air, a silent symbol of the endless wonder of magic. "Zordeya and Whistluss have a long history of loyalty to the fortress of The Winter King, meaning anyone tasked with defending it needs to be assessed."

"More lessons?" I ask, glancing at the fine strings of gold forming the Deyewinn's temporary wings.

"Questions more than lessons," Eaiwin replies, offering me a smile. With her weave of sparkling hair lifting in the wind, she adds a little more. "Questions about commitment and your potential reaction in critical situations."

"Life-threatening ones, you mean?"

"Yes, Guppy. I'm sure you saw the visions in the water."

I nod, deciding to watch the others gliding in the sky alongside our girl guides.

"Your collective journey will end soon, which is when the ..."

"Pilgrimage begins," I interrupt. "A pilgrimage to prove ourselves to Taeia, putting him back on his rightful path: the path towards a kingdom."

"Yes. The visions will continue to form, sometimes in mirrors, other times in water and so on." Eaiwin adds.

"Helping to guide us along the way."

"Yes."

"And the Jacqus will appear when life hangs in the balance?"

"Along with the might of Zordeya."

"For now, it's time to part the clouds and guide you on — until we meet again."

And then she's gone, stepping off our Deyewinn into the open sky, falling elegantly with the other girls.

"Now what?" Conrad asks as we glide towards the parting clouds.

"We make our way through," Kaira replies, moments before our magical birds return to their liquid state, leaving only a lace of gold wrapped around our feet. Kaira's calm response suggests she's travelled here before, looking down as the laces of gold fall in a vertical line, like strings attaching us to an invisible world.

It's a new sort of tightrope walk I'm happy to experience,

watching as the strings stretch below us — a farewell gesture from a golden bird able to morph in and out of existence.

"It feels like we're back in Zilom," Lucy says, looking down at the bridge of gold decorating the sky.

"Pretty cool," Noah adds, attune to any suspicious movements above the clouds.

"Are the Whistluss army similar to the women of Zordeya?" I ask Kaira.

"They're less intense," she replies.

"But they're as brilliant in battle?" Conrad checks.

"Elegant and devastating."

"That's good to know," Jacob adds, deciding against a handstand this time. "So, how do we get into Whistluss?"

"Our Quivvens mainly," Kaira replies. "They'll release themselves in a while, pushing out from under our skin."

"Why?" Lucy asks.

"Material magic," Kaira explains. "Our Quivvens are the thing we'll use to climb higher, forming a connection of allegiance between worlds: sort of like blind flight."

It's enough of an explanation to satisfy us, waiting for the moment when our Quivvens break free.

"So, where is Whistluss exactly?" Conrad asks, checking to see if his Quivven's moving under his heart.

"All around," Kaira replies with a smile.

Conrad offers Kaira a frown, realising patience is required.

"I can't see anything but clouds," Noah adds, leading us to an obvious conclusion ... that we're already in Whistluss ... a realm hidden within a mountain of clouds.

"I think I'll stay a bit longer," Jacob comments as his Quivven stretches beneath his skin. "This is a *lot* more fun than teaching The Fateful Eight."

"The fun hasn't started yet," Kaira adds, smiling as her Quivven frees itself from beneath her wrist.

"When you say *blind flight* ...?" Noah queries but our Quivvens provide the answer, piercing through our skin until they're hovering near our faces. "Grab on and close your eyes," Kaira instructs, "and don't let go."

I grasp my Quivven in my hand, closing my eyes to let its magical powers flood my vision. There's a world in every cloud, full of creatures and wise women.

"*Looks cool*," Conrad says, sneaking a kiss in before we take off.

It's a subtle touch of love I appreciate, but I also know it's his way of drawing me into a race. We've abandoned our morning flights to lead a rescue mission, thoughts of the magical world we've left behind always close by.

Conrad's already off, tumbling through the sky momentarily before he works out what to do, sensing the laces of gold provided by the Deyewinn are part of this ritual. The strings of liquid magic attach to his Quivven, running through small holes in the brass artefact, forming a zipwire between where we are and want to be.

"Yes!" my boy wizard shouts as the Quivven melts into the palm of his hand, forming a loop he holds on to as he whizzes along. It's all the encouragement we need to join him, waiting for our laces of gold to connect us to a city of clouds.

Conrad wants a race, all right, so I swing my legs forward to increase my speed, whizzing past Jacob and Noah with Lucy keeping pace. I forget about the visions I saw in the water guiding me up here, realising I'm powerless in the face of destiny.

There are pilgrimages to survive and Bloodseekers to navigate, but that seems a million miles away as we whizz through the skies, our penchants glowing in the palm of our hands as we chase Conrad, heading to a land of warriors of a different kind.

———————

THE MOUNTAINOUS CLOUD WE FLY INTO PROVIDES THE entrance to a realm dominated by white pillars and strange butterflies with long tails, accompanied by small, frail women who don't have the look of warriors. I made the mistake of judging a Society legend by her stature a few years ago, paying the price for my ignorance with a public humiliation.

I'm not going to make the same mistake this time, choosing to study our new surroundings, leaving questions until later. Clouds transport people in Whistluss, operating as platforms to their desired location. The women move through the cloud barrier filling the space between the white pillars, talking to their butterfly companions as they do.

I'm keen to explore but know the etiquette in new places, beginning with welcome gestures and establishing purpose. The purpose part is mostly out of the way, but like Mylisia said there will be questions to answer here.

"Welcome," comes the voice of a woman who appears through the clouds, dressed in a silver garment. Like her compatriots in Zordeya, she's barefooted and regal in her own way although lacking the obvious power of Mylisia and her crew.

A silver butterfly floats above her shoulder, its long, black tail motioning its own welcome: a gentle touch on each of our wrists.

"You've learnt something of Zordeya," the woman

continues, "and we will do our best to offer similar gifts: the ability to dance with death and more."

"Nice to meet you," I reply, not knowing what else to say as a collection of clouds pass by with passengers on them.

"Likewise, Guppy Grayling. You and your friends have a long, arduous journey ahead of you so rest and recuperation will be needed."

I nod, glancing at the others as the silver butterfly (that isn't really a butterfly) stretches out its tail again, this time towards a passing cloud.

"Please, step on," the frail lady says, joining us as we do. "Your bedrooms have been prepared."

"Do the butterflies understand what you're saying?" Jacob asks, naturally drawn to the way the women communicate with their companions.

"It's the other way around, Jacob" the lady replies with a smile, her thinning hair resting on her shoulders. "It is for us to understand that language of Whistluss creatures: a language formed in every move and gesture."

"Wow," Lucy utters as more inhabitants appear through the cloud barrier filling the gaps between the tall, white pillars. "Does it take a long time to learn?"

"A lifetime."

"Do you know all our names?" Conrad adds, wondering if it's a good idea to stroke the silver butterfly keeping us company.

"Yes, Conrad," the lady calling herself Krieala replies, "and now you know mine. Your gift of flight will help you on your pilgrimage, as Jacob's affinity with magical creatures will his."

"I haven't got a gift," Noah comments, reaching out to touch the passing cloud.

"Perhaps you need to be tested to uncover it."

"Maybe."

"Kaira is a Renn so has the gift of water reading. Do you see much in the water, Kaira?"

"A struggle to free Taeia from himself," Kaira replies cryptically as we float along.

"Your first battle in the skies has gone to plan, although things will be not be so straightforward on entering Kelph."

"There's an army waiting for us," I comment.

"An army in many guises, Guppy, leading to the main reason for your journey here: access to our sacred balm bringing soldiers back from the brink of death."

"Does it always work?" Lucy asks as we pass through the cloud barrier, entering into a section of bedrooms resting on carpets of cloud.

"If used in time, yes although timing is the critical factor. Death will cling to you at opportunity, so knowing when you're about to cross the bridge between life and death is the art you're here to study. For now, though, it's time for rest and recuperation. I will leave my companion with you. She will provide privacy once you've chosen your rooms. Dinner will be waiting when you wake."

With that, our frail host exits on her cloud, leaving the silver butterfly to flutter nearby as we choose our rooms. They're a surprisingly normal set of bedrooms with a bath resting in the middle of each one. I need a bath, that's for sure, and a little alone time with Conrad.

I'm wondering how much privacy a wall of clouds gives you, thinking about the dinner on offer later on. Krieala thinks we all need sleep but I'm wide awake, parting the clouds behind the bed to look out onto a peaceful Whistluss sky.

"I'll take the double bed," Jacob says as he flops down on

it. "I'll need to head back in the morning so need my beauty sleep."

"Decided to give another battle to the death a miss?" I joke, stepping into the bedroom next door with Conrad.

"No funny business," Jacob teases. "I doubt the walls are soundproof."

"I'll try to keep Guppy off me," Conrad replies with a smile.

"I'm going to sleep in the bath," Noah adds, looking a bit worse for wear in his blood-stained chinos and ripped cardigan: marks of battle from earlier.

Lucy falls onto another double bed, staring up at the wonder of a hotel in the sky. Kaira hovers between rooms, studying us all for a moment as the silver butterfly rests on her shoulder. "It's something the creature does to check our need for privacy."

"Then what?" Noah asks.

"Then she'll call more of her kind — four for each room — and they go to work forming walls of silver, decorated by their bodies in each corner. Just let the mottlefly know when you're ready."

"I'm full of energy," Noah replies.

"Wait until you get in the bath," Kaira says with a smile, offering a wave before she heads to her bedroom. I miss my time with her, staying up all night in our room in The Cendryll, but I also know that time has gone. We're older now and wiser, understanding what Society duty gives and takes.

I worry she'll take the same path as her dad and aunt in the end, anchored to a magical world to the exception of all others. She's still got us, of course, but as things change she remains the same in some ways: kind, gifted and burdened by the name Renn.

"Well, a bed of clouds isn't bad," Conrad says as he runs the bath for me.

"A bath of clouds is better," I reply with a quick kiss. "You can always join me."

"I thought you'd never ask."

I stroke the mottle fly as it rests on my shoulder: a signal for the walls of silver to be activated. "There you go, we'll wait for their touch of magic and then I'm all yours."

"I haven't heard that for a while."

"We've been a bit busy."

"Love and war," Conrad sighs in a comic manner. "The life of a Society soldier."

"Well, let's get back to the 'love' bit while we can."

"Let's hope the walls hold up," Conrad says as he returns the kiss, pulling me towards him as the wall of steel appears around us — the four mottleflies decorating the corners like Kaira said they would. "Do you think they're watching? It would be a bit weird if they were."

"They look frozen," I reply, sensing no movement in the winged creatures. "Come on, let's see what Kaira means about the water making you sleepy."

"I'm wide awake and ready for action."

I laugh at this, turning the taps off as Conrad reveals his scarred torso: a sight I don't tire of.

"How's the wound?" he asks, inspecting the small scar on my neck.

"All healed up."

"I wonder when my blood mark will draw an attack."

"Sooner rather than later, probably, but we're focusing on love not war, remember?"

"Well, your lover boy's ready," Conrad replies, deciding to leave his jeans on as he wrestles me into the bath, falling asleep minutes later. There's something in the water, all right.

———

THE PEACE OF WHISTLUSS IS SURPRISING, NO SOUND penetrating the steel wall. My mum's the first person who enters my thoughts once Conrad's asleep. It's a recurring vision I have of her, sitting by the window in a twisted building, wondering where her son and daughter are.

I've done the usual avoidance thing again, making excuses for not seeing her. It's less about blame these days because I'm learning to forgive, like I promised Jacob I would.

The sound of my brother's snoring reminds me of one more thing: his point about Taeia never being wanted. Jacob was the one who looked after me when our mum chose power over parenting. He also took Kaira under his wing when she arrived in the S.P.M.A., his compassion stretching to a life-threatening intervention on The Hallowed Lawn.

He put his life on the line to save Taeia then, but might not be around this time. He's got responsibilities in The Cendryll, leaving it to us to save a desperate boy from tragedy. I wonder what turned my mum towards a dark path as I settle in the bath — the realisation dawning that if I can't work this out, I've got no chance of turning Taeia away from his descent into destruction.

Thinking about my mum again, I consider the questions we need answers to. What does it mean to be completely alone, marginalised to the point of contempt? What has fuelled Taeia's low sense of self-worth? Finally, why does he hate us so much?

"Good night, mum," I whisper, struggling with a sudden

surge of emotion. After all, I led the pursuit of my mum when I knew she'd put the S.P.M.A. in danger. Could I have done things differently? Would it have changed anything?

More importantly, can I find a more compassionate path this time? A way of protecting the sky realms without shattering the spirit of a boy who's already broken.

11

A LEAP OF FAITH

I wake up in warm water with Conrad's arms around me. It feels like we've been in the bath for ages, but it's hard to tell because we're in a windowless space. There's no daylight in the rooms, the silver walls still intact with the mottleflies static in the four corners of each one.

Whatever's in the water did the trick on Conrad, whose loving intentions slipped away from him within minutes of entering the bath. I'm still fully clothed, my black leather trousers and matching top soaking in the warm water. It's one way to get clean, I suppose, but I want the comfort of a bed so I nudge Conrad awake.

"Hey, lover boy ... time to wake up."

Conrad mumbles as he holds me tighter, clearly not wanting to leave the warm water. "I've only just fallen asleep."

"You fell asleep straight away — so much for love over war."

"Well, I'm awake now and ready for action."

"Too late, Casanova; I need to get out of these soaking clothes."

"Be my guest," he adds with a familiar smile.

"I've got nothing to change into."

"Precisely."

"Too risky and weird with those butterflies watching."

"They're hardly watching."

"How do you know?"

"So, we just lie on the bed until we dry?" Conrad asks, looking unimpressed with the idea.

"Something like that, giving us time to work out how we get Taeia to see sense."

"A few more pirates circling in ice graves might do the trick," Conrad comments as we get out of the bath and fall onto the bed. "The faster we get moving to Kelph, the better I say." Conrad continues lying alongside me, the scar running from his neck to his waist always drawing my interest.

"Agreed and let's hope he doesn't end up like my mum."

"You can't keep punishing yourself for that. You were thirteen, Guppy and your mum could have destroyed the S.P.M.A."

"I still wonder if I could have stopped her. She's got nothing now."

"Your mum turned her back on you; what other choice did you have?"

I shrug, crossing my arms as I adjust my position. "I've been thinking about her more since we've been up here ... how *alone* she is now. Taeia's alone in the same way, searching for acceptance in the wrong places."

"He'll only get worse when the Kelph elite reject him."

"Yep."

"Do you think he's ready for what's ahead?"

"He better be."

A KNOCK CAUSES THE MOTTLEFLIES TO FLUTTER INTO ACTION, their tails running from the corners of the steel walls, creating narrow gaps which Kaira looks through.

"Dinner's ready," she says with a smile before adding, "It's usually better to bathe without your clothes on."

"Very funny, Kaira," I reply, wondering if there's some simple magic to dry our clothes.

"You probably want to get changed into these then," Kaira adds, showing us some grey garments.

"They look like sacks," Conrad comments, grimacing at the sight of them.

"Sacks or soaking clothes," Kaira replies, expanding the gaps in the silver walls with a rub of her forefinger. "The mottlefly's power is in its tail — the main thing we'll be learning, apparently."

"What about the life-saving balm?" I ask.

"All in the tail. Come on, everyone's waiting for us."

WITH A CHANGE OF CLOTHES — THE GREY GARMENTS TURNING out to be surprisingly comfortable trousers and a top — we're back on a cloud joined by Krieala and a host of mottle-flies. We glide between the white pillars until we're in a different space with moving hexagons on the floor, turning like clockwork. The dining table's at the end of the room, looking out onto the faintest vision of enemy territory.

"Where's the food?" Noah whispers as we step off the cloud onto solid marble.

He's got a point; there isn't any food on the table and I'm *starving*.

"Check under your robe," Lucy teases as we reach the table, a comment on the ill-fitting clothes Noah's wearing.

With a sarcastic smile, Noah checks under the dining table, hoping to see food floating there: he's disappointed again. Conrad and Jacob are more interested in the marble floor, hexagons rotating anti-clockwise as we take our seats at the table fit for a king.

We're in the realm of queens, of course, although it's been a very different experience to Zordeya so far. A gold palace, gold armour and the ability to whip thunder into shape with your *hair* makes you pretty royal in my book. Whistluss is a quieter affair, making me think the power here lies in wisdom rather than a warrior code — wisdom we're yet to learn more about.

Once sat at the table, the food appears from the rising marble tiles, presenting us with trays of hot and cold food: salad and Sunday roast being the ones we all go for. The above-ground world has its limitations but Sunday roast isn't one of them. Cakes appear afterwards which are devoured as our frail host looks on, not eating a thing as the mottleflies perch on the edge of the table: silver creatures with hidden powers.

My attention's drawn to the faint outline of sky towers in the distance, the unmistakable outline of Kelph looking a little too close for comfort. The women who join us at the table don't look concerned at all, asking us if we've had enough to eat before discussing what Krieala described as 'the ability to dance with death'.

WITH THE FOOD CONSUMED, THE MARBLE TILES FUNCTIONING as trays return to the floor, replaced with others that rise for a different purpose ... the inside formed of glass containers filled with liquid. The mottleflies find their way into the glass containers and our education begins.

"How did you sleep?" Krieala asks as the liquid darkens, mirrored by the light in the sky outside.

"Fine," I reply, studying the mottlefly closest to me, its tail whipping against the glass.

"They're not being hurt, are they?" Lucy queries, looking uneasy as the silver creatures stop moving.

"Not at all," comes another voice — older with translucent skin and long, white hair. "Remember, Whistluss creatures lead us; we can only learn from them."

"So, do they influence the sky as well?" Jacob checks. "The way the light's faded with the colour of the liquid."

"In the same way the throne of Devreack belongs to The Winter King, the skies of Whistluss belong to its creatures."

"And they're teaching us something now?" Conrad prompts.

"Yes, Conrad; the mottleflies are teaching you the art of humility."

That only brings a puzzled look to Conrad's face, but Jacob's onto something, applying his unique affinity with magical creatures.

"We think the mottleflies serve us but, in truth, we serve them," Jacob states, stepping off his chair to get a closer look at each silver creature. "They're pretending to be helpless while controlling the sky's tone and rhythm: a sign of their secret power that is easily underestimated."

"Like Taeia's," I add, catching on quickly. "He hasn't shown us his full power yet, making him more dangerous."

"The mottle fly is our gift from Whistluss. First of all, however, you need to know its key weapon."

"The tail," Jacob replies.

"And how can you tell?"

"We can't. Kaira told us."

"So, how are you going to identify Taeia Renn's chief weapon?"

This brings a silence to proceedings. It's an obvious question we've overlooked. We know what Taeia *can* do, calling lightning to him like a long-lost friend, but that's *all* we know. He's got limited powers but beyond controlling lightning *what are they*?

"Can you tell us more about their tails?" Kaira asks as the mottleflies begin to move in their liquid cages, silver specks floating in the water.

"We only learn by following," Krieala explains, gesturing for us to step onto the tiles. Pillars of glass form stretch through the clouds until we're impossibly high, perched on pedestals in an open space.

"Simply follow," the Whistluss women say in unison, perched between us as the mottleflies break free of their glass cages, releasing the liquid as they do … liquid that fades as quickly as it forms.

The second thing to fade are the creatures themselves, their wings matching the colour of the sky until they're invisible. It's the reason I don't see their tails whipping out at the frail women, lacerating their skin and sending blood into the air. The blood doesn't fall but rises, the women showing no signs of pain as they remain perfectly still on their pillars of glass.

Their calm state doesn't change when the expected visitors arrive … Bloodseekers who move towards the women. The fact our hosts don't prepare a defence suggests it's part of the lesson, allowing the blood running down the white pillars to draw the vampire army towards them.

The lesson increases in intensity when the first line of

Bloodseekers are caught in a razor sharp attack ... the mottleflies' black tails whipping at their throats, covering them in their own blood.

The remaining Bloodseekers last a little longer, jumping from one blood line to another until they're blinded by a swarm of silver dust coating their eyes, bringing a shriek that rings through the air.

"They're like Mantzils but in a good way," Conrad says to me, referring to the mind-bending creatures haunting Quibbs Causeway.

We're in no real danger, the creatures who rule this kingdom flaunting their powers until a strange thing happens ... they become visible again ... wrapped in the lines of blood drawn from the women of Whistluss. They remain static in the air, drawing the surviving Bloodseekers towards them ... powerful creatures allowing themselves to be shredded by venomous nails.

The sky falters when this happens, turning blood-red until I remember what the women said to us: simply follow. Following means falling into battle. I don't even check my theory, launching myself off my glass pillar with a whisper of 'Levenan'.

I use my arm to release a flood of water around the floating blood until it's under my control: a defensive wall between me and the Bloodseekers turning to attack.

"Guppy!" comes the sound of Jacob's voice as my brother leaps into the air, followed by Conrad and the others.

The lesson, it seems, is the magic of humility and it starts here, surrendering to the lords of Whistluss in their moment of need: a sacrifice of ego to save something precious.

The wall of water holds up long enough to be reformed into a Velinis charm, the dual protection of water and

colourful energy helping to keep the Bloodseekers at bay —
unless I *need* to be attacked to earn the most sacred thing on
offer here: a balm giving me the ability to dance with death.

"Defence, Guppy!" Conrad shouts as he flies through a
tunnel of ice, but the mottleflies' shattered bodies continue
to fall, and I follow.

Kaira's alongside me moments later, spinning in her own
Velinis charm. "Your bubble of protection won't hold for
long, Guppy."

"I know."

"Do you know what you're doing?"

"I hope so. We have to earn the right to the elixir of life,
Kaira, and it's earned in blood. The blood bond we made
with Thylas: proof of our commitment to the cause. Why
would we be offered life without risking our own first?"

"You've got a split second to get it right," Kaira advises as
our bubbles of protection falter under the vampire attack.

"Get Conrad and the others in position," I reply. "I'll give
the Bloodseekers an open strike then we take them out.
Freeze them in ice graves for me."

"Will do."

As another cry of "Guppy!" rings in the sky, I prepare to
put myself in the firing line, reassured by Kaira's reaction
who's been here before. There's also no sign of panic in the
faces of the frail, grey-haired women watching from the
pillars of glass: wise witches overseeing a familiar ritual.

The attack happens in a split second, nails ripping at me
as I remove my protective force field ... just long enough to
give the army of Bloodseekers hope. It's enough to draw the
necessary amount of blood from me, leading my Night
Ranger crew to do the rest and they do it with ease, turning
water into ice to end the argument.

I'm weakening rapidly, struggling to reactivate the

Velinis charm as I fall into the broken bodies of the mottle-flies, their wings sticking to me on contact. Conrad and the others surround me, using the Magneia charm to form a carpet of clouds beneath me.

"You bloody idiot!" Conrad shouts, rubbing his skin as his attempt to reach me backfires, the broken mottleflies still powerful enough to dictate things. "What are you trying to prove?"

"How we escape death," I reply as the creatures' tails turn white, settling over my wounds as the bleeding slows. Fragments of their silver wings cover my penchant bracelet, the blue gemstones glowing brightly as my blood turns silver ... glittering silver running through my veins until I'm free of pain: a sign we've found the way to activate the elixir of life.

All it took was a leap of faith and a lesson in humility — a lesson Taeia needs to learn before it's too late.

12

EYE OF THE STORM

With a lesson in humility complete, our pillars of glass return us to the sanctuary of Whistluss, the mottleflies who healed me fluttering nearby, fully recovered from their own rescue mission. It's a new bond formed, reinforcing the principles of beauty and unity we live by.

It's good to know we'll have another spectacular creature nearby, the sense our mission to Kelph is now imminent. We step off the platforms that lifted us into the sky, the hexagonal tiles returning to their position on the marble floor.

With the tiles rotating like clockwork, I wonder what else they can do, checking my new wounds for any evidence of scars but they've completely healed.

"You could have been killed," Conrad says, "taking a risk like that."

"I just followed the women's lead."

"No, you *guessed*," Jacob adds, echoing Conrad's point.

"Adapted."

"And if it'd been a mistake, Guppy?" my brother asks

"You would have raced to my rescue."

"Your old impulsiveness is coming back at the wrong time."

"I thought you had to leave," I counter, getting a little annoyed by the lecture.

"Jacob's right, Guppy," Conrad states. "We can't go jumping into enemy lines on a hunch."

"We can if the mottleflies are there, which is the point I was trying to make. Our blood marks are future wounds we can't avoid, so we're entering different territory now. *All* of us are going to be wounded — some of us critically — so we need to get used to the idea of being outnumbered and outgunned.

We don't have the upper hand in this battle; the advantage is with Taeia because he's got royal blood whether he likes it or not. The Kelph elite don't want him taking the throne, and they *definitely* won't want us interfering so they're going to swarm us on entry: the point where we're forced onto separate paths."

"So, the creatures are going to be our guardians," Lucy comments, stepping alongside me in a gesture of support. "The mottleflies, Williynx and Jacqus when they appear?"

"Right, Lucy. We've always needed help on our missions, and we're going to need it *a lot* more on this one. Like the women of Whistluss have said, the creatures reign here, meaning they probably reign in other sky realms as well."

"Sounds like we're going into battle blind," Noah adds, deciding to stand still on a white tile, enjoying the simple fun of being rotated anti-clockwise. "Not that I'm complaining. We've still got our Quivvens which help us to fight blind, along with our understanding of material magic."

"We'll have help from a lot of places," Kaira states, checking the wounds on my arms, "including the sky soldiers from our world."

"My uncle?" Noah queries, clearly surprised by this thought.

"Yes, Noah: your uncle, Sianna and Sylvian Creswell."

"I thought Sianna had given up fighting," Conrad comments, keeping a close eye on me as the women of Whistluss give us some space, realising their part has been played: the time for battle is upon us.

"She likes to think so," Kaira replies, "but she's taken up a critical position in The Royisin Heights, suggesting otherwise. Sianna's hideout is the secret sky tower there, and remember her closeness to Thylas?"

"Almost like a disciple," I say.

"Thylas has a loyal army scattered through the sky realms," Krieala says, returning our attention to the frail crew sat at the dining table. "Whistluss and Zordeya are part of that band of 'disciples' as you put it."

"I didn't mean to offend."

"No offence taken, Guppy; it's a natural assumption to make. We fight to defend a kingdom, after all, in the same way you protect yours. Like you, we've given our lives to defend what is sacred to us, making us all disciples in a way — disciples to a way of life rather than any individual — a way of life you've also become accustomed to."

"Does it ever get old?" Jacob asks, deciding it's polite to re-join our hosts at the table.

"Magic never gets old, Jacob, principally because of its perpetual wonder. A lifetime wouldn't show you its depths or capabilities, something worth defending we believe."

"Me too," my brother offers with a tired smile: a sign it's time for him to return to Society duty.

"Any of the tiles will take you back," Krieala explains to my brother. "A simple case of asking."

"Really?" Noah prompts. "You can get back to the

S.P.M.A. from here? I thought you had to travel through the skies."

"Not the S.P.M.A. but a safe space between our worlds. Returning alone through the normal channels is inadvisable. This option puts Jacob on a flight path towards Zilom, ensuring a safe return to his teaching duties."

"It sounds like you know a lot about the S.P.M.A.," Conrad comments as the wall of clouds part, offering an outline of familiar sky towers: a shadow of Kelph awaiting our arrival.

"Each world interacts with others," Krieala explains. "It's the way of all magical universes. Think of us as planets aware of each other's existence, keen to understand the boundaries of our existence."

"Do you still fight?" Lucy asks.

"We orchestrate when necessary," another woman replies, "following the rhythms of the skies which determine all things: the very rhythms calling Taeia as we speak."

"He can still be saved," Kaira says, sitting alongside me.

"Agreed," Jacob echoes, unsure of what to say to be transported back to The Cendryll. "So, I just ask to go back?"

The women nod, leaving Jacob to work it out for himself. The Entrinius spell doesn't work and neither does saying his destination.

"What about the Quij?" I suggest, knowing Jacob's ability to call the creatures in times of need.

He nods his understanding and closes his eyes, muttering something I've never been able to make out. The Quij don't appear but multi-coloured lines do: a sign contact has been made. I stand to give my brother a quick hug, wishing he could stay. Every goodbye could be the last, after all.

"Don't do anything stupid when I'm gone," he says, letting me go as the marble tile drops a few inches.

"You know me," I reply, waving goodbye as he drops further down, returning the wave before the rings of colour fade and he vanishes into the darkness.

———

JACOB'S RETURN SIGNALS OUR OWN DEPARTURE, WAITING TO see if the marble tiles are going to take us on, but no such luck — our journey continues in the sky. We find our clothes washed and dried in the rooms we slept in, thankful for the gesture.

Slipping into my black, leather trousers, I run my hand over my skin where scars should be, smiling at the magic of the mottleflies. I just hope their life-saving touch will be available in the future, something telling me I'm going to need it again.

All that's left to do is say our goodbyes, offering thanks to the women who orchestrate in war, making me wonder if Whistluss is the resting place for fading warrior women: a transition from liquid gold to peaceful white.

Either way, each army has unique powers at their disposal and I'm happy to call them allies. We're going to need as many allies as we can get now, because the time's come to step into the unknown, sensing the enemy waiting in the wings.

As we travel with Krieala on a cloud, ready to make our exit, she offers one more piece of advice. "You were offered the gift of gold in Zordeya whilst witnessing the healing benefits of silver here. The Deyewinn has blessed you with luck and the mottlefly will return you to life. Death is waiting for you all so trust in what you have learnt, and beware all that is offered from this point onwards."

"Use our Quivvens to test the measure of all offerings," I say, remembering what Sianna taught us in The Royisin Heights.

"Indeed, Guppy, because there are no more allies to meet — only enemies with armies of their own."

"Do you know when we separate?" Conrad asks, rubbing his copper-blonde hair as nervous energy runs through him.

"On arrival," Krieala replies. "The reason a mottlefly will travel with each of you ... until you reform as one."

"Shame we haven't got our Williynx for company," Noah says, tapping his feet nervously.

"Some of your feathered friends remain in Kelph, trapped under a curse which can be lifted with your penchants. A touch of recognition will return the Williynx to you. First, trust your mottleflies to guide you and *nothing else*. Bloodseekers abound in Kelph and our boy-king is ready to send his own welcome message."

"Not friendly, I imagine," Lucy adds with an intensity in her eyes — our pixie witch ready for her first taste of all-out war.

"A statement of intent," Krieala explains as the cloud we travel on takes us between two white pillars and out into the open air once more. "The good news is mottleflies' tails have more than one power: they can carry companions as they fly. Their silver wings will coat with a layer of dust as you take off — not to heal but to hide you from prying eyes."

"Cool," Conrad says with a smile, brushing my arm as he prepares for battle flight.

"I will bid you farewell here," Krieala states. "Remember, trust what is known and *nothing else*."

"Thank you," Kaira says, buttoning her velvet jacket as

we prepare for take-off. "You've given more than we could have asked for."

"Only what you have earned, Kaira. Now, I can only wish you well and remind you that the skies are aligned to pure intent, never bending to the will of a king out of time."

With that, Krieala steps onto a passing cloud, the frail woman who welcomed us saying her goodbyes as we reach for the tail of our new companions: mottleflies ready to guide us into battle. We're whipped upwards on contact, the shot of energy rushing through my arm as a blanket of silver dust falls onto me ... just as Krieala said it would.

The dust hovers around my body as we rush towards the silhouetted sky towers in the distance. It's comforting to know we can't be seen, hanging onto our companion's tails with both hands. Liquid-gold armour will be the next thing to activate as we close in on Kelph, my mind returning to the golden bird who assessed our fate in Zordeya.

The Deyewinn pecked at my blood mark, inspecting me until Mylisia explained my fate was unclear. As far as I can see, there are only two possible outcomes to this rescue mission: death or destiny restored.

13

DESCENT TO KELPH

The descent to Kelph is trouble free, no sign of familiar enemies as the mottleflies guide us on, an invisible silver shield protecting us from sudden attacks. Luckily, I can still see enough to make out the Gothic towers we fly over — the place where Taeia's holed up with his black Williynx and soulless army.

Then again, maybe it isn't that obvious and our hollow king is on the move, drawing us deeper into Kelph where things are likely to get messy. The surrounding silence isn't a good sign, our silver-winged companions gliding above the towers and bridges suspended in the sky — none of them housing people sympathetic to the cause.

We're in the land of pirates with a *very* different agenda. Our mottleflies decide to descend lower, easing us onto the pinnacle of the towers decorated by windows and flags: a statement of intent to the Kelph elite who stay hidden.

There's no light in the windows this time, another sign of a battle brewing. I remember our first trip here with Thylas Renn ... how two lines of sky soldiers glided through the air on lines of fire... silent soldiers known as the Axyiam, arriving to show their respects to a fading Winter King.

The Kelph elite sat on stone thrones then, hovering in mid-air that stretched towards us. Charms were used to create thrones of our own, beginning a conversation to assess the enemy.

The meeting ended dramatically when no reassurances of peace were offered, sending Thylas into a fury and the Kelph elite scattering as the Axyiam swarmed us: an inferior army easily thrust aside by a king with a point to prove.

We stand on the sky towers, studying the bridges that swing from side-to-side, offering no clue to who's watching. They're watching, all right, including Taeia wherever he is.

"Where is everyone?" Noah whispers as the mottleflies rest on our shoulders, their black tails raised like antennae attuned to danger.

"Holding their fire probably," Conrad replies, touching the Quivven glowing in his neck. "Looks like they're using their own invisibility charm," he adds, "because the buildings look empty."

"Or they've scarpered," Lucy suggests, "knowing what's best for them."

I check my own Quivven buried beneath my wrist, wondering where the first attack will come from. The silence and emptiness are a simple touch of sorcery: a clever move under the circumstances. Taeia's made his opening statement — that we're in enemy territory — unlikely to get out of it unscathed.

"Where are you hiding, Taeia?" I whisper as the bridges lift towards us. They're black bridges with no sign of life, adjusting their position until they connect to the Gothic towers we stand on: a welcome of sorts.

"It begins," Kaira says, throwing her Vaspyl into the air to create two weapons: scythes decorated by silver dust.

I understand the statement, having prepared for this moment for a while now: the moment our own pilgrimages begin to gain the trust of a boy out of time. Releasing my own ball of morphing steel, I transform into two swords: my go-to weapon in the eye of the storm. A gift of silver settles on the swords, ensuring the combined powers of our magical worlds are activated.

"We're walking into a death trap," Noah comments as the bridges swing in front of us, our Quivvens illuminating the silent towers and buildings below.

"All in a day's work," Conrad replies as orange energy surges from his hands, his silver-winged companion wrapping its tail over the scar on his neck: a sign of unity as the bridges flare into life.

"Remember what Krieala said," I remind the others. "To trust what is known and accept nothing else."

A nod from everyone is the signal to begin our personal pilgrimages, stepping onto the flaming bridges with weapons at the ready. Invisibility is an option for us as well, but something tells me it won't have the same power here. We've arrived to gain Taeia's trust so hiding our moves isn't the answer.

It puts us at greater risk which is the point, putting ourselves in the vulnerable position he's always been in — out of place in a world we don't belong in, hoping to navigate our way to peace. There's a storm within Taeia, though, symbolised in the flaming bridges that mark the start of combat.

"See you on the other side," Conrad says to me with a familiar smile. It's the phrase he uses before our morning flights in the S.P.M.A, something that feels like a distant memory right now.

"We come to the aid of anyone in trouble," I reply, keeping my swords raised as I step onto my flaming bridge. "No one abandoned on the battlefield."

"Assuming we get there," Kaira adds, activating a Velinis charm as she does. With silver dust coating her bubble of protection, she adds, "We're on our own for a while now: a test Taeia's put in place for us."

"Meaning we can't save each other," Lucy states, blinking tears of gold into life … the trick needed to activate her liquid-gold armour.

"Probably not," Conrad replies.

"Well, it's only a flaming bridge and a few thousand pirates to sort out," Noah jokes, always keen to lighten the mood. Activating his own gold armour along with rings of protective fire, he adds, "Easy work for Night Rangers."

"I admire your confidence," I reply, studying the blood mark appearing on my left wrist.

"Well, we've got mottleflies with life-saving balm and sparkling, blue Jacqus to get us out of trouble, so what have we got to worry about?"

"That?" Lucy replies, pointing at the sight of an army appearing on the other end of the bridges: a familiar army with vengeance in their eyes.

"The Axyiam," I mutter, remembering the mildly human faces marked by slits for eyes.

"They don't look very friendly," Noah adds, rethinking his 'easy work' assessment.

"The good news is they can't see us," Conrad comments. "They work on scent."

"Well, let's put them off our scent," Kaira suggests, uttering 'Comeuppance' as she produces a Zombul. "Jacob can produce Quij by blowing on his hands, and we can do the same with one of these."

"Good thinking, Kaira," I say as the Axyiam step onto the bridges, chanting as they move through the flames.

"We just need the silver dust of the mottleflies' wings to make it work. So, I say we take out our Zombuls and release a flurry of Quij," Kaira continues, her silver-coated scythes glimmering in her hands. "The moment they sense the enemy, they'll turn blood red which is when we move in, obliterating the threat before we move on to the next test."

"Taeia's little game," Lucy comments, following Kaira's advice and producing the steel artefact decorated with holes.

"A delicate game we have to tread carefully in," Conrad replies, remembering the lesson in humility learnt in Whistluss. "We have to stick to the mission whatever he throws at us, because he wants us to quit or try to take him down."

"Reinforcing his lack of self-worth," Noah adds, following the rhythm of things. "It's his party now."

"Correct," I echo, "so let's have some fun before we extend our invitation."

And the fire dance begins.

———

WITH THE QUIJ RELEASED AND BUZZING IN FURY, WE MAKE our way across the flaming bridges suspended in the Kelph sky ... light appearing in the Gothic towers as they do ... more windows illuminated below as battle begins. As the bridges begin to swing more violently, the pirate army storm into action, fooled by the scent of the Quij hovering above in a wall of colour.

The Axyiam close in, hovering above the surface of the bridge to storm down on the enemy, but they're met with a rival army of subtle movements and blistering force ... a Society army that targets their faces ... burning and ripping at the skin to disorient the senses.

Additional fire comes from the mouth of the primitive crew, incinerating a small number of Quij, but the majority dodge the fire, reforming above before attacking in brutal synchronicity.

Kaira's already moved in on her swinging bridge, using her scythes in a boomerang fashion ... an effective way of doing damage without putting herself in the firing line. It works perfectly, the attack aimed at the bodies of the Kelph soldiers, struggling with the combined force of a human and creature army.

Kaira's bubble of protection is holding up against the flames, its silver-coated outer layer the steel binding magical powers together. The pirate army that break through fail to penetrate Kaira's protective shield of light, ripped apart by the Quij that grow in number as the Zombuls release more, our silver-winged companions looking on for now, perched on our shoulders as the first stage of battle rages.

Having the ability to camouflage themselves in the environment, the mottleflies are under no threat, recognising this as a crude attack that's easily extinguished. So far so good, I judge, glancing at Conrad, Lucy and Noah as I transform my two swords into longer blades, spinning as I rip through the wounded pirate army flying towards me.

The Disira charm works a treat as I vanish out of view, re-appearing above the enemy to end the argument. My swords extend and retract, puncturing the Kelph soldiers as the Quij target their faces, the flaming bridges doused with water by Lucy and Noah as Conrad blasts his way out of trouble ... sending a dozen Axyiam flying through the air ... their shattered bodies dripping with blood.

"LEVENAN!" comes the combined shout from Lucy and Noah, directing a surge of water at the stranded enemy — quick thinking to avoid another problem appearing: Blood-seekers.

As the blood of the broken dozen is washed away, the mottleflies go to work for the first time, leaving our shoulders to add their own touch to proceedings. A gift of silver that closes the show — silver dust forming into liquid steel that races through the air towards the necks of the surviving Axyiam, throttling them into submission.

With an army defeated and our bridges free of fire, a combined magical force rests for a moment, checking the skies for the arrival of further threats, but none appear ... the black bridges swinging more calmly now as more lights appear across the landscape.

I don't know if this is a sign of recognition or impending retaliation, but it doesn't really matter either way because the real journey hasn't begun. The Quij take care of the dead in Society tradition, releasing threads of colour to wrap the bodies in. It's a mark of respect I suggest we should show to the enemy — another sign our intentions are to restore peace.

As the bridges settle, we watch the Quij lower the dead bodies over each bridge, releasing more colourful thread to guide them towards the ramshackle buildings below. Whoever lives in these isn't linked to the Kelph elite hiding in the towers behind us.

They might be caught in the crossfire of conflict here, or maybe foot soldiers ready to be called into battle. I hope it's the former because if it is the tide will turn against Taeia sooner than he thinks.

He's lost soldiers in Zordeya and now more in a realm he claims as his own. Hiding can only last for so long whatever the strategy is behind it. As the first sound of thunder rumbles through the sky, we survey the landscape of Gothic towers and burning bridges again, wondering when a king is going to show his face.

"The bridges are collapsing," Conrad says, pointing to the sight of black dust lifting in the wind. "It's time to move."

Our silver-winged companions respond, lifting us into the air moments before the swinging structures disintegrate, showers of black dust falling into the pit of a pirate economy protecting their new leader.

"Good luck," Lucy says as we glide over the collapsing structures into a no-man's-land of trouble, knowing our personal pilgrimages are about to begin.

There's nothing else to say as we fly off in different directions, recognising survival is in our own hands now.

14

A BOY OUT OF TIME

As I begin my pilgrimage to prove my worth to an ex-comrade I can't stand, I let go of my mottlefly's tail, recognising the need to rely on my own powers as the dust of battle is behind me. I decide not to turn back and watch the others fade into the distance, knowing it's time for tunnel vision if I'm going to survive the next test.

If Taeia's watching, he better be ready for another run in with a Fire Witch. King in waiting he might be, but anyone who hides behind an army, watching comrades fall at every hurdle, is no king of mine. With my silver-winged companion gliding above me, I blow gold dust into the air, using my penchant stone to direct it under my feet: Zordeya's gift of gold coming in handy now.

Fighting blind becomes a necessity as my Quivven spins beneath my skin: a sign of trouble. A whisper of 'Verum Veras' protects me within a glittering curtain of light as I glide on my pathway of gold, deciding to rely on old tricks instead of new ones.

Old habits die hard and I'm confident Society charms

will improve my reaction time, as long as they're coated in the magic dust released from my mottlefly's wings. I'll leave the liquid-gold armour for another time, knowing I've got life-saving balm at hand if the tide turns against me.

"Come on, Taeia ... where are you?" I whisper as more Gothic towers appear in the distance, these ones bursting through rocks lining my route on either side.

Lights go on in these towers as I get closer, my Quivven spinning faster as it illuminates the interior of the towers. Vast halls flood my vision ... spaces empty of life except for one lined with mirrors ... the reflection of Taeia Renn in all of them.

It might be a trick to draw me in, but there's only one way of finding out so I tilt to the right, kneeling as I change course, heading beneath the clouds towards a tower fluttering with a black and red flag: a black Williynx forming the crest in the middle. Kelph has captured a sacred Society creature and a boy-king's soul, but not for long if I get my way.

Remember, trust what is known and nothing else.

The words of a frail warrior woman echo in my mind: Krieala's final advice before we left Whistluss.

"It can't be this easy," I whisper as I close in, allowing my Quivven to direct my course at it rotates slowly, operating like a compass in an enemy realm.

Part of me is expecting bullet rain or more Bloodseekers, but neither appears as if the whole of Kelph is under Taeia's silent influence — the same influence that put Jacob's students into a zombie state only a few weeks ago. If he *has* put his army on hold, essentially freezing enemy fire to observe our personal pilgrimages, it suggests he's gaining more power.

Controlling pirates and Bloodseekers is one thing, but

the sky is too silent all of sudden … the bridges in the distance resting in a strange state of calm. From the looks of things, I'm going to fly into the sky tower housing mirrors unchallenged: a sure sign my troubles lay within.

No burning bridges or chanting Axyiam this time, just some thickening mist to navigate which my Quivven does with ease. It's time to prepare my defences as I reach the window of the sky tower bursting through the rocks, wondering what trick Taeia's got up his sleeve as the window loosens from its frame, offering me a platform of welcome I refuse.

Nothing can be trusted now aside from our Society training and the gifts provided in Zordeya and Whistluss. This pirate realm has already tilted a boy wizard off course, looking to do the same to me, but I've been here before and I intend to be here again, so it's time to see what the mirrors have to offer.

———

WITH THE WINDOW RETURNING TO ITS FRAME IN THE SKY tower, I touch down in the centre of the vast hall, remaining within the protection of the Verum Veras charm until I know more. I'm not stupid enough to make the first move, waiting to check if Taeia's actually here. Whether he wants us dead or not is up for debate, but the Kelph elite definitely do and I've got the feeling they're part of this party trick.

The huge mirrors lining the walls remind me of the ones in Zordeya — mirrors that assessed my wound before the golden Deyewinn took over. Maybe these do something similar, identifying my weaknesses instead of my wounds: psychological or physical scars maybe.

It's time for patience … no sudden moves as my mottlefly

rests on my shoulder, its tail pointed to the mirror in the corner of the vast hall. I pay more attention to this reflection, studying Taeia who appears in each mirror, looking like a narcissist who's obsessed himself.

"It's rude to stand on ceremony."

His voice echoes through the hall, increasing in volume as it penetrates my protective curtain. It reminds me of the Mantzils' power ... a mind-bending force causing me to reach for a vial of Liqin.

I gulp it down quickly, keeping my eyes closed as I decide to respond to the comment, using the Magneia charm to pull the mirrors away from the wall, watching as they crash to the floor.

"Always impulsive," Taea replies, echoing in my head again but a Weveris charm takes care of this: small webs protecting my ears from the destabilising sound. With my mottlefly's tail still pointing to the corner of the room, I decide to reveal myself, confident it will draw Taeia out if he's here.

"I told you I belong here," he says, feeling closer now, "and that I didn't want any part of your world, but here you are anyway, blinded by your loyalty."

"That's right," I reply, readying the Promesiun charm as my Quivven points in the same direction as the mottlefly's tail. "Loyalty and bravery, Taeia, something you seem to be struggling with."

As the shattered glass moves towards the corner of the room, I blink gold armour into life, deciding it's time to rely on Zordeya magic.

"You confuse bravery with stupidity, Guppy."

"Well, I'm standing in the open and you're hiding out in a tower," I reply, directing the Promesiun charm towards the moving glass fragments, keen to feel the power of an old comrade. "It reminds of the time you hid in the trading lane, after you'd turned a mild curse on us.

You were crying then — maybe you're crying now after watching your bridges burn and comrades lowered into the abyss."

"Pirates that *worship* me!" comes a more familiar tone as Taeia appears, formed from the fragments I'm trying to pull away from him.

He looks like a god, that's for sure, his features fully formed as he moves towards me, lifting his hands towards the windows that explode seconds later ... glass daggers flying towards me as the the ceiling crashes down.

The Fora charm takes care of both as my silver-winged companion keeps Taeia occupied. Its tail shreds as it connects to his shimmering figure, sparks flying off him as it does. With the shattered ceiling and windows circling around me, the expected happens ... more trouble in the form of a wind storm that lifts me off my feet.

The wind pulls me towards the shattered window frames and an awaiting enemy in a different guise: the leaders of Kelph working in tandem with their new leader. Taeia lets out a bitter laugh as he explodes from the fragments, muttering something that freezes my mottlefly in mid-air — moments before it's obliterated with a whip of his arm.

With the sacred creature blasted into dust, I'm about to go the same way as I'm overwhelmed by the wind storm, flipping upside down as I smash into a window frame, succumbing to a single act of sorcery from a boy wizard with vengeance on his mind.

The Disira charm doesn't work because I can't speak, blasting the Promesiun charm towards the shattered tower in a last-ditch attempt to stay alive. My Quivven's still working though, rotating more erratically as it attempts to drag me out of the firing line.

I've got enough energy to send multiple Spintz charms into the air — the SOS call taught to us by Farraday for times like this. If Sianna's right, the Jacqus will come to my rescue: the beautiful, blue bird that explodes into a crushing force field in the face of danger.

As I shake my head to clear my vision, the Kelph elite fire out, perched on stone thrones in a circular formation, making the point that I'm out of my depth in a realm fit for a king.

My body smashes into the sky tower as my left leg snaps at the knee, an invisible force field crushing me as the leaders of Kelph look on ... unmoved as my Promesiun charm dies ... a sign my time's up as another blow shatters my left arm, drawing a howl of pain from me.

It's *impossible* to move against the combined force of Taeia and the elite army he's formed, recognising pirates and Bloodseekers won't do the trick. My last thought as I lose consciousness is the hope that the others are alive, battling their way along their own paths, fighting the good fight as life drains from me: a Fire Witch finally meeting her match.

A dream of blue floods my vision as I drop through the sky, feeling like I'm sinking under water as the light in my Quivven dies. It's not what I thought death would feel like, but I'm moving in and out of consciousness now, watching a circle of stone thrones collapse into one another.

The Kelph elite vanish out of sight as the wave of blue lifts, painting the sky in a statement of intent: the realisation dawning that my SOS call has been answered.

15

RHYTHM OF WAR

I wake up on the golden wings of a Deyewinn, looking
up at a familiar face. An army of warrior girls glide
through the sky, surveying the territory from their
golden companions' temporary wings.

We're not in Zordeya or the cloud world of Whistluss,
but the shimmering blue surroundings of Jacqus at work:
the Society creatures who came to my rescue as Sianna said
they would.

The blue shield of protection suggests the enemy's
hovering on the horizon, waiting for us to reappear. The
power of the Jacqus is keeping them at bay, and I imagine
the warrior princesses are making them think twice.

From what I can gather, the Kelph army respond to the
call of Taeia Renn whereas Bloodseekers scavenge wherever
the dead and dying rest. Taeia's retreated again, using
charms to mask his movements, vanishing seconds before
the Kelph elite were blasted into the skies along with their
stone thrones.

The dust of battle will settle and the hunt for an apprentice king will continue, but for now I've got wounds and

absent friends to worry about. I check my arms and legs to see strings of gold wrapped around them: a magical bandage applying healing properties to broken bones. Well, they *were* broken but not anymore.

All I've got now is a tight sensation in my joints, but Eaiwin tells me this will pass in time: the caramel-skinned warrior decorated in gold.

"The first phase has begun," Eaiwin says, offering her hand as I get to my feet.

The strings of gold around my wounded joints tighten as I stand. "The phase where I almost fall at the first hurdle, you mean."

"The phase of Taeia's retreat," Eaiwin replies. "The Axyiam and the Kelph elite blasted into submission, and skies littered with ice graves and burning bridges. He isn't the king they hoped he would be, realising what they've always known: that only one king reigns in the sky realms."

"The Winter King."

Eaiwin nods, surveying the quiet skies.

She reminds me of Kaira more and more, making me wonder if she's another Renn burdened by fate. Sparks stretch out from her weave of hair, acting like sensors assessing potential danger. It's an impressive sight to see: Zordeya girls dominating the sky on golden birds as battle halts.

She said this battle was their first test — proof of whether they were worthy of a life in Zordeya. I've got a feeling they're going to pas this test. The question is will I?

Bending my wounded joints to accelerate the healing process, I ask about Conrad, Kaira, Lucy and Noah. "Any news on the others?"

"Safe and well so far."

"No one else injured?"

"Not seriously."

"I'm sorry about the mottlefly."

"War comes with many casualties, Guppy. Mottleflies, like all magical creatures, live and die to protect their sacred universes."

"I was too slow to react."

"Taeia was too powerful for you: the reason he's put you all on individual paths."

"Giving him more chance of defeating us?"

"Of course," Feweina interjects, gliding closer to me — the giggling girl who's locked into warrior mode now. "He isn't a killer and he's losing his shallow army. Now, he's battling to avoid his fate, retreating as the throne of Devreack begins to spin."

"Which means?"

"Dead kings are moving to force destiny upon him."

"Dead kings?" I query, lifting my arms as the Deyewinn tilt to the left, following the streaks of sparkling light directing our flight path.

"When the throne of Devreack spins, every aspect of the sky realms feels the vibrations. The skies offer everything in our world, including the power to stop time. When that happens, Taeia will find himself facing his ancestors: the only army he can't defeat."

"So, he's running out of time."

"Yes," Feweina replies, standing proudly on her Deyewinn's wings. "He's surrounded by forces closing in on all sides, having no idea how to atone for the chaos he's caused."

"He's always been lost — like someone else I know — never fitting in and falling foul of the rules."

"Well, the rules are different now," Eaiwin states, sending out a battle cry to her comrades, "because our boy-king is in a battle with time, and time submits to no one."

"So, it's do or die?"

The girls gilded in gold nod, lifting their right arms to signal strike positions. "The throne of Devreack is calling," Feweina explains, "and every member of the sky realms will have to answer when it does."

Pointing ahead, Feweina adds, "We're about to be swarmed by weather creatures and sky soldiers: retaliation for the Jacqus' attack on the Kelph elite."

I nod, readying myself to return to battle in the hope I'll fare better this time.

"Imagine you're back in your world, Guppy," Eaiwin advises, "fighting on solid ground with a trusted army by your side. The Deyewinn will be by your side throughout, like a Williynx would be. It will respond to your every move, working alongside you to offer protection and guidance. Trust *both* worlds — the Society's and ours — it's your only chance of survival."

I nod again, understanding exactly what this means. I've been hesitating until now, second guessing my every move, fearing I'll make a critical mistake. With a Williynx army behind me, I would have found fluidity by now, moving to the rhythms of war like I did before. These rhythms need to be found soon before more blood marks appear, marking future wounds I might not recover from.

Weather creatures carry the pirate army this time, winged creatures formed of lightning and fire as a storm of bullet rain flies towards us. With a new army alongside me, I prepare to re-engage the enemy. The shower of sparks released from the warrior girls' hair halt the momentum of the initial attack, long enough to move me in position.

Remembering Eaiwin's advice, I lie flat on my golden

Deyewinn, imagining it to be my trusted Williynx. With a wall of electricity forming, climbing higher in the sky, the second stage begins: the race to the top of the wall to reach the enemy on the other side.

As the Axyiam climb higher, nearing the top, The Deyewinn make their move, melting into the electricity field. Seconds later, we're faced with a fountain of liquid gold, fusing with electricity to create a beautiful monster.

Golden lava drips from the fountain dominating the sky, under the control of warrior princesses as it falls over a desperate enemy. Some escape the counter move but many are caught in the eruption, screaming as their bodies are coated in boiling hot liquid.

With the fountain pouring lethal fire on a fractured force, I turn my attention to the creatures formed of fire and lightning. Born from the elements, they seem to have second-guessed our first move, circling as they prepare to release their own blistering attack.

I've learnt how to capture lightning, using it as a form of travel — the form of travel I choose now as I activate the Magneia charm, drawing the creatures towards me. It's an obvious move on its own, but with more Deyewinn flying into view there's more to the plan ... flying towards the enemy being part of it.

A look from my Zordeya comrades suggests I might have taken the 'trust' thing too far, but intuition and split-second timing got me through the last war, so I close my eyes as the Quivven rotates beneath my skin, directing my course as my vision is flooded with enemy lines.

As my golden companion races towards me, I activate a Spintz charm to add some light to the party, mainly used to disorient the creatures carrying the surviving Axyiam. It's enough to put me in position, circling on a stage of lightning bolts as I pivot with the expected attack: clouds of fire and lashes of lightning flying towards me.

I move beneath the pirate army as the Deyewinn's wings forms a protective shield around me. The plan is to station myself behind the Axyiam army with a creature full of magical charm. It will only take a second to construct another stage of gold.

The creation of choice is a golden tower, similar to the ones surging from the floor of Whistluss. A battle tower will give me a panoramic perspective of battle, working with my Zordeya army to set another trap.

A signal from Feweina urges me to get to work forming our new theatre of war: a glittering colosseum courtesy of the Deyewinn's ability to melt in and out of existence.

Lightning and fire surge towards me but I dance out of danger, using the Verum Veras charm to protect me as I stretch layers of gold into the shape required. I've finally found the rhythm of war, moving to the places my Quivven lights up, the dots guiding my war dance.

All it needs now is the young Zordeya army to test their warrior credentials. Turning into tornados of light, they swarm the enemy, absorbing a sea of bullet rain as they do. With one wave of attack neutralised, I fire a Promesiun charm towards the lightning creatures heading my way.

Their fragile frames shatter on impact, leaving only the surviving Axyiam floating in the colosseum of gold: soulless soldiers about to join their comrades in gilded graves. It isn't over yet, though, signalled by the sight of black Williynx circling above.

We managed to release some from their spell on the boundaries of Zordeya, and I see this is a chance to do the same. My position on top of the golden colosseum makes me an obvious target, but there's no one riding the cursed Williynx, something I don't completely trust.

I've never heard of a Society creature attacking its own kind, but I'm in different territory with strange sorcery at work. It's better not to take a chance, I decide, knowing what a blast of Williynx ice can do.

With the warrior princesses looking on, I stand on top of the colosseum as more coffins fill the sky. All that's left to do is attempt another rescue mission, exchanging counter fire for healing touches.

"Over to you," Eaiwin says, joining me on top of the colosseum. "The Williynx will respond to your call."

"What call?"

"What do you normally use to call them?"

"A Spintz charm if we're in danger."

"A shower of light," Eaiwin explains, "similar to the energy field we used to free some of their kind. Pure creatures will always respond to pure magic, Guppy. Williynx belong to your world, after all."

Reassured by the confident looks I'm getting, I utter 'Spintz', lifting my right arm towards the sky. Williynx are a pure breed, after all, responsible for protecting the most sacred source of magic in the S.P.M.A. With more Spintz charms added to the blanket of light, I breathe a sigh of relief as the darkness drains from my feathered friends, returning them to their former glory.

I watch as they rise higher, releasing a shower of colourful feathers in a gesture of thanks — free of the captors who imprisoned them.

16

A STORM OF LIGHT

With the skies free of enemy fire, I return to a more familiar form of travel courtesy of a fire-red Williynx. It's a reassuring feeling, realigning yourself with a creature that's done so much to guide and protect you.

From the look of the young Zordeya army, standing proudly on the wings of their golden companions, no other attacks are likely leaving me to ask about my friends again.

"Each of you has help on your journey," Eaiwin explains, reaching out to stroke the yellow Williynx gliding alongside her.

"So, no one's been seriously injured?"

"No. You have the will of the winds on your side."

I still worry about Lucy and Noah, mainly because of their inexperience in war. If they're navigating battle successfully, it's a good sign. I have different concerns for Conrad and Kaira. As skilled as they are, we're battling against *elements*, some of which are not under our control."

"When will I join up with the others again?" I ask, watching the revitalised Williynx soar in the sky, blasting out streaks of ice for the hell of it — or to warn any waiting threats what's in store for them.

"When the time comes," Feweina replies, staying alert as she throws her hair over her shoulders.

The Gothic towers and swinging bridges aren't too far away so I enjoy my time perched on my Williynx, confident in my ability to avoid danger in its company. As stunning as the Deyewinn are, my connection with a Williynx is much stronger: a bond created in my formative days in the S.P.M.A.

"The swinging bridges are about to propel another enemy into action," Eaiwin explains, pointing at the black structures that gather momentum. "The bridges act as a portal protecting them from view; we have a plan to draw them out."

"Which is?"

"Obliterating the bridge from a distance," Feweina replies. "The small buildings below function as weapons as well as dwellings. The closer we get, the more danger we're in so expect to be bombarded from all angles."

I check my Quivven, happy to see it glowing again as it rotates slowly, the glow fading to an arrow pointing east. "What's in that direction?" I ask, pointing to the dark cloud bank hanging where my Quivven's pointing.

"The Hollows," Eaiwin states. "Almost certainly where Taeia's retreated to ... a cloud atlas of multiple portals only seasoned warriors have entered."

"A maze of death, you mean?"

"Always so dramatic, Guppy Grayling," Eaiwin replies with a familiar smile. "Sky creatures know our world better than any human — even a king in waiting — so we put our trust in them once we enter The Hollows."

"So, we smash the bridges and take out the enemy, clearing a way to the cloud maze?"

Each girl nods, waiting for me to lead the way. I've got a point to prove after being rescued earlier, and there's no better introduction to battle than a blast of ice. Not a single strike but a co-ordinated one, dipping to my left as I orchestrate a collective storm to smash the enemy out of hiding.

The sound of the bridges shattering cracks through the sky, sending black fragments flying into the air, accompanied by a different breed appearing through the carnage ... not Bloodseekers or pirates ... but an army covered in hair and oil, entirely focused on their prey.

Within a minute, the strange breed circle us, riding on the fragments of a bridge that's morphed into its own weapon, flying towards us like shrapnel as the lizard-like crew strike. Whatever they are, they're powerful and agile, spitting strings of venom as they leap from their floating stages.

The venom looks like phlegm, suggesting they're riddled with disease — a curse they're keen to share with us. I dip below the gathering storm, holding tighter as my fire-red Williynx uses brute force to engage a new enemy.

As a co-ordinated attack turns the flying fragments into dust, more problems appear as a Deyewinn gets caught in the cursed phlegm, melting into liquid gold as it does. It's transformation doesn't free it, though, unable to release itself from the cursed chains that discolour it.

Two more Deyewinn get caught in the crossfire, their temporary wings melting away as they're caught in mid-attack, followed by two warrior girls being struck by the cursed bile moments later ... their faces melting as the phlegm latches onto their skin, causing a shriek of pain and a howl of victory from the enemy.

It's my turn to offer protection, leading a Williynx charge from high up, guiding the majestic creatures to release strings of mist to halt the strange sorcery. The two girls are horribly deformed, failing to extend their liquid-gold armour over their faces in time, their eye sockets sinking lower as they lose their battle for survival.

I manage to flood the lizard army in a prison of their own, a fire charm trapping them in their cursed phlegm. It's enough time to weaken the sorcery, freeing the girls as I activate the Weveris charm, black bile flooding from my mouth … venom of a different kind.

With the deformed warrior princesses grasping at their faces, I direct the black bile towards the fireballs, shifting the momentum in our favour. The bile coats the fire prisons, blinding the reptilian army as the warrior girls take over.

A storm of lightning obliterates the swarm of enemy fire — revenge for their injured comrades who float helplessly as a flurry of mottleflies appear, coating the girls in silver dust to make them invisible to the eye.

With the Zordeya sky coated in the debris of battle, the threat decreases, allowing the injured girls to bathe in the mottleflies' healing magic. Out of harm's way, the girls rest in death-defying balm. The remaining threat is taken care of with a combined blast, the surviving few slowly sinking in their own bile.

The creatures continue to spit their venom, realising too late they're being flooded by their own poison. They've underestimated unfamiliar magic: Society spells laced with a touch of sky sorcery — every bit as fatal as their weapons.

"We send a signal to The Hollows now," Feweina says with a rare ferocity. "A statement of intent to our apprentice king."

"Are the girls going to be okay?" I ask, keeping the enemy trapped in their cages of fire and black bile.

"The mottleflies will restore what they can; a Yaxl curse is permanent once it attaches to the skin. The Deyewinn lack the might of the Williynx; they are vehicles leading us into battle, ready to offer their healing magic when necessary."

"Why didn't the girls extend the armour over their faces?"

"Inexperience," Feweina replies as her weave of hair spins upwards. "The speed of a Yaxl attack is surprising, made harder to defend due to the flying fragments used to disorient the enemy."

"Maybe a Deyewinn can help with their injuries?"

"Yes, to a degree, but first we need to send a message to your boy-king, readying him for retaliation."

"Just say when," I reply, wondering what sort of statement Feweina's got in mind. It looks like the surviving lizard army are going to find out soon enough.

Like a lot of creatures drawn to darker rhythms, they're primitive in looks and actions, unable to adapt in critical situations, howling as they swipe helplessly at the balls of fire surrounding them.

The Weveris charm was a statement of its own, showing the feral lot and anyone else watching that Society magic is beautiful and brutal.

"On my command, deactivate the fire but leave the black bile active," Feweina states. "We can do the rest."

I nod, my body burning with the power of Society magic flooding through me. It's a reassuring feeling to know I'm getting the hang of material magic, helping me rediscover the split-second timing needed to survive battles like this.

It's this timing I draw on now as Feweina begins a chant,

stamping her feet with the other girls as lightning rips through their hair, streaking towards the creatures who fly free as I release the cage of fire.

The black bile stays in place as instructed, connecting with Zordeya lightning as the enemy tries to flee. Gold comes next as the Deyewinn fly into the lightning blast, melting as they do until a guillotine of gold is formed ... an enormous blade stretching across the sky as it rips through the retreating creatures, creating a canvas of blood in the sky.

It's sudden and brutal, sending the intended signal to an apprentice king with a distaste for death. His shallow army is dying in significant numbers, written large across the sky realms: ice graves near Zordeya and gilded tombs suspended in Kelph.

The concluding act is the letter of intent Feweina wanted, the severed bodies propelled towards The Hollows. The Zordeya army lead this act, their hair wrapping around the severed torsos as a chant fills the air ... eyes closed as if they're calling on the skies to infuse them with thunder.

The sky realms stay silent as the dead are propelled east — the position my Quivven still glows in — hurtling towards the location housing the boy I first met as a Night Ranger. I imagine Taeia looking on, watching his army crushed at every point, maybe wondering if life in the S.P.M.A. was so bad after all.

"THE MOTTLEFLIES WILL DO WHAT THEY CAN," EAIWIN explains, sensing my unease as the girls are attended to.

We're sitting on white benches in a temporary portal, created by a parting of the air. The Williynx guard each end, maintaining imposing forms as the all-girl army rests. The two injured girls are covered in the mottleflies' life-saving balm, a coat of silver dust covering their deformed faces.

It's hard to watch — the sight of such young, pretty faces permanently scarred. I'm hoping the golden creatures hovering nearby can add their healing touch, like they did with me. When they do, a feeling of relief rushes through me. I know their wounds are permanent, but at least their faces have been constructed to some degree.

"What happens to them now?" I ask, careful to keep my voice lowered as the healing ritual continues.

"They heal and fight on," Eaiwin adds matter-of-factly, taking a seat alongside me.

"What about their vision? Their eyes, I mean?"

"Their vision will be restored; their faces scarred for life. Some venom is beyond the magic of beautiful creatures, Guppy — just as it is in your world."

The Terrecet, I think as Feweina says this: the lethal arte-fact scarring numerous Society soldiers in the last battle. Farraday's one of the scarred survivors, watching from the wings somewhere along with Casper and Philomeena. I wonder how long it will be before they make an entrance.

"They knew the risks and accepted them, as you have done."

Studying my Quivven, I ask, "Can you tell me more about The Hollows?"

"They are formed of connected sky towers," Feweina explains.

"Like a maze," I comment, watching the Deyewinn drip more liquid gold on the girls' faces.

"In a way, yes. Each tower opens out into an expanse of space. The spaces shift with the energy of the occupying force: a jigsaw puzzle designed to protect whoever's inside.

Plus, any of the spaces can be accessed by any part of Kelph, meaning our apprentice king will be able to draw on any additional firepower he chooses."

"Giving him the element of surprise."

"Yes, Guppy but that's not all. Like the bridges that burned at the start of your journey, the towers are creatures too. Each one is a potential prison. Legend states that many have perished in the towers, their silent screams muted by the spell cast within the spaces."

"Sounds ideal," I quip, my thoughts turning to Conrad and the others.

War was the furthest thing from our minds a few months ago, but magical universes have their way of surprising you. I mean, who would have thought I'd be putting my life on the line again, trying to save a boy-wizard with a God complex?

As that thought fades, Conrad and the others return to my thoughts. A Follygrin's no good up here and my Quivven only illuminates the realm I'm in. I wonder if Williynx feathers have got more magic in them, glancing at the colourful birds who remain stationed at either end of our sky portal.

"Here," Eaiwin says. "Tea for the senses."

"Thanks," I reply, taking the cup of warm liquid. I sip the tea, enjoying its sweetness. There's no magic in it except for the calming sensation it provides. At least that's what I think until I peer closer, squinting to check if I'm imagining things.

'Tea for the senses' is a perfect description of the strange brew warming my hands, offering the faintest reflection of my Night Ranger crew. I watch as each of them moves through strange locations, weapons at the ready with familiar comrades by their sides.

Conrad moves in a shield of tanzanite light with Sianna Follygrin by his side: our host in The Royisin Heights who's returned to Society duty. Noah rides a path of lightning with his uncle — the meticulously dressed Aarav Khan who forms an arc of light with his right hand, illuminating the vision of sky towers ahead.

Lucy's walking under an arch of white light, accompanied by Sylvian Creswell: the wizard I met in The Goronoff Mountains. It was the first time I'd seen the sky realms come alive, studying the quiet man who stood bare foot alongside Kaira, waving her off as she spiralled upwards, laying the ground for our meeting with a Winter King.

Kaira walks with the figure I expected to see up here eventually — Farraday returning to protect the girl he's looked out for from the beginning. Help has been offered to us all as Feweina said it would, and since Farraday knows more about the sky realms than he's letting on, he's probably the best guide Kaira can have.

Ravaged by the last war, our old friend and comrade draws a laugh from Kaira as an army of mottleflies surround them, maybe conscious of the fragile state the Society legend is in.

"Go well," I whisper, studying the flickering image, happy to know they're safe for now ... on a journey towards a maze of death.

Although it's not clear this is their path, it seems obvious in a way — all roads lead to Taeia Renn as the world closes in on him.

TAEIA'S RECKONING

With the faces of the two warrior girls reconstructed to some degree, we sit in two lines in our sky portal, preparing to engage the enemy again. The benefit of this protective portal is the way it moves through the sky like a silent juggernaut.

I speak to the injured girls who sit together, sparking golden spears into action. It's clear they've got retaliation on their mind, the map of scars across their faces making them look more fierce than ever.

They tell me the pain's minimal and that vanity has no place in a legendary army. It's enough to make me park any ideas of sympathy, struck by the way they return to thoughts of battle.

The Deyewinn stay close to them, dripping liquid gold into their hands. Instead of putting it on their faces, they drink it — another way of administering remedy, it seems. At least they haven't lost their vision, blinking through bloodshot eyes.

If anything, they're stronger now ... battle-hardened and clinical in their thoughts ... here to win a war and end a boy-king's inner conflict. The Hollows are where we'll meet Taeia again — a maze of connected sky towers under his silent influence. It's a moving monster of a different kind, protecting its prized asset as he sinks deeper into the recesses of Kelph.

In a way, the pirate kingdom is a symbol of Taeia's mind: dark and unanchored. Maybe it's the reason they were drawn to each other, a lost boy sensing an affinity with hollow kingdom. The Kelph elite made their position clear in our meeting with them, stating they would offer sanctuary should it be requested.

What they *didn't* mention was how they worked to influence Taeia's mind, sending signals via sky channels that he began to interpret, until whatever he sensed on top of The Cendryll's skylight became clear. The statement from the leaders of Kelph was the trigger for Thlyas' reaction: a final statement of power from a king in the grips of death.

Another cup of tea would go down well, allowing me to watch the others on their journey. It's hard fighting with the people you love, even harder when you're forced onto separate paths. Like all things in war, though, you have to adapt and avoid self-pity: the dead should be pitied, not the living.

"We're closing in on our destination," Feweina says as the Williynx flap their wings in readiness. "We'll enter through the same tower but that's where our unity ends."

"What do you mean?"

"Imagine the sky towers as a shifting beast, attempting to trap you in its lair. Once we enter, it will move ... every part of it. The towers are a key form of defence in Kelph. Unlike most realms here, however, they lack a blessing from the skies, making them vulnerable to attack."

"A strange place for Taeia to choose," I add, "stepping into a shell of protection we can penetrate."

"The move of a desperate wizard, giving the shifting towers the chance to trap him in his own mind. After all, if they can sink an heir to the throne, psychologically at least, they weaken the power of Devreack."

"Which helps them to ravage other realms," I comment, seeing through the crude plans of pirates.

"Yes, which is what we plan to stop," Feweina replies before adding, "We're here."

Gothic towers dominate the sky ... ten times the size of the others decorating the Kelph skyline. They also rotate slowly, the flags decorating each tower flapping in the wind. The towers are formed in a quad, slate tiles connecting them in with no additional buildings visible.

It's a maze all right and one I'm about to jump into, ready to meet an ex-Night Ranger for the second time in a few days, hoping for a better outcome. As the towers continues to rotate, a narrow window comes into view again: the sign to jump into action.

I ride with my fire-red Williynx again, watching as the warrior girls decide to travel on pathways of gold. The Deyewinn glide nearby until we're through the windows, rising to the top of the towers as we do, acting as a look out for enemy forces on their way. Entering the sky tower is different this time, unlike my last experience that ended badly.

There are no mirrors lining the walls but doors instead — as if the Taeia is mocking The Society that offered him salvation. The doors swing open and closed — like they do in The Cendryll — offering portals to other places. Something tells me what's hiding behind them isn't going to be welcoming.

Like Feweina explained, the towers are moving monsters ... shifting illusions designed to disorient people considered a threat. As the doors clatter open and closed, tempting me to make a false move, I keep my Williynx close, activating the Weveris charm to form a black web around me.

The aim is to stay visible, remaining in the firing line but remembering the scared faces of two warrior girls — the consequence of momentary inaction. Like always, Society magic is marked with sky sorcery, blowing a mouthful of gold dust within my web of protection.

"Hold your ground," Eaiwin whispers as the Zordeya army take their positions, forming a line in front of the doorways.

Protected by their liquid-gold armour, weaponry is formed in the shimmering spears first appearing in our sky portal. Their hair acts as a secondary weapon, charged with lightning as it spins above them, having the power to control lightning and twist thunder.

The first sign of enemy fire is a subtle movement ... a gust of wind blowing through a door in the west corner of the space ... gentle wind that flows through the room ... a trick we don't fall for.

I've got my Zombul in my right hand, the silver artefact able to release vicious creatures in a flood. As the movement increases, I tighten my grip on the Zombul, ready to introduce vampire birds to a similar breed: Bloodseekers who are likely to be waiting in the wings.

With the wind turning to mist, the first blast of battle sends me into the air ... the Kelph elite returning to finish me off. They haven't legislated for the power of a Williynx, though, caught in a swarm of red feathers that give me the seconds I need.

I open the lid of the Zombul to release a blizzard of my own — the shrieking introduction of the Ameedis. The vicious creatures swarm the leaders of Kelph, ripping at their skin and hair as the proud group of witches and wizards fight back, trying to obliterate the vampiric birds into dust.

So far, there's no sign of Taeia but I know he's here, hiding behind a wall of protection as he always does — some Winter King he's going to be. His aim is to limit the army pursuing him, I imagine, hoping most of us are taken out before we reach him, making his concluding act easier.

There are other problems waiting behind the clattering doors … wind followed by sweeping rain and twisting thunder, threatening to drag us through a doorway until the warrior girls release their fury, spinning in mid air as golden spears fly from their hands. The spears morph into rectangular shields, covering the doorways closest to them.

I follow suit, directing my protective black web towards the closest doorway — the liquid web holding strong as thunder tries to rip it free. So far so good on our journey through a maze of death, unable to create prisoners of us yet.

With the doorways blocked, the room begins to stretch, floorboards snapping beneath our feet as we're faced with a revitalised Kelph elite, bloodied and focused on revenge.

Blood will draw the expected company soon enough, but until then a duel begins the new rhythm, adults and teenage magicians facing off against each other, each protecting what's sacred to them — sacred being a loose term for pirates with no moral compass.

"Draw them in," Eaiwin says, "then use their own weapon against them."

"Which is?" I ask.

"Every fragment used to attack us: floorboards, windows and shattered doors."

I nod, glancing at my fire-red Williynx who blasts out a

sheet of ice, replacing the floorboards as they splinter and circle around us. The Kelph elite look on contemptuously, confident they've caught us in a trap, but we've got a Williynx for company and golden Deyewinn standing guard outside.

As the splintered floorboards swarm around us, I prepare the Fora charm: the force field used to halt the momentum of attacks. A static defence got me in trouble last time, though, so I prepare my own version of bullet rain in the form of steel bullets.

My Williynx adds its own fire power as the battle begins, a wall of wooden spikes flying towards us as the ceiling collapses — a co-ordinated move to catch us off guard — but the Fora charm takes care of the ceiling, halting a rain of slate.

I take advantage of the pause in action, skating on the sheet of ice to close in on the enemy, signalling for the warrior girls to do the same. My move is helped by the appearance of mottleflies ... hundreds of them releasing a shower of silver dust into the space ... the advantage we need to regain a foothold in the conflict.

As I ready myself to weaken the leaders of Kelph further, Taeia Renn makes his entrance. He's dressed in a long gown, making him look like a clown prince. Surrounded by the half-blind Axyiam and reptilian Yaxl, he looks on with a nervous smile.

With Taeia in my peripheral vision, I inch forward across the floor of ice, protected by a magical gold armour and silver dust, my face wrapped in rings of fire courtesy of the Infernisi charm. The flying wooden spikes bounce off me, disintegrating as they do, the distance between the competing crews closing by the second.

A sudden blast intensifies the action as the doors fly free

of their constraints, a blizzard of gold and silver meeting them as mottleflies, Deyewinn and a girl army shower Taeia's party with a co-ordinated attack.

The magical birds have no trouble with the reptilian army's cursed phlegm this time, remaining in fluid form as they blind the Yaxl with golden lava ... blistering them into submission: revenge for the scars left on two warrior princesses.

Amidst all of this, Taeia looks on, shrouded in a robe that protects him from counter fire. He stands perfectly still within the storm, unmoved as various shrapnel sinks into the robe: magical armour for the occasion.

Once again, he doesn't try to inflict fatal harm on anyone, the nervous smile marking his face suggesting he realises his predicament: trapped in a maze he's made for himself. Like us, he's going to have to battle his way out, no longer the all-powerful heir he entered the pirate economy as.

He's failed to overwhelm those tracking him, limiting his ability to close in on Devreack. More than ever, he's a boy out of time uneasy in his emperor's clothes. With his pirate crew writhing in pain on the floor of ice, he watches me pivot out of danger — the one witch he's desperate to bring down.

It takes a shower of steel bullets to make him react, the smile faltering as he counters my move, sensing it's more of a familiar dance than a lethal strike. He whips out his left hand, sending the fire-red Williynx crashing into the wall, creating a clear path to me: it's time to dance.

Deciding to add his injured comrades to the casualty list, Taeia lifts the badly burnt Yaxl into the air, turning the twisting thunder on them, their melting bodies spinning above him.

With the Kelph elite looking on, caught in a moment of doubt, the injured Yaxl are directed towards them at furious speed, followed by lines of lightning that penetrate their defences: an unexpected betrayal they didn't see coming.

Silence fills the shattered space for a moment, Taeia studying his work as he stares at me. Glass and slate still hovers above us, the very thing he turns his attention to now. With his own comrades splintered into silence, he decides on his next move, confident in his power to end this once and for all.

He ignores the cloud of mottleflies surrounding the injured Williynx, equally unconcerned by the Deyewinn that melt into the ice floor, forming a battle line between us. Exactly what this is going to achieve is unclear, still an apprentice in a new kingdom, standing opposite its heir.

"You really should have learned your lesson," Taeia says, studying the warrior girls who form a line alongside me.

"What lesson's that?" I ask, watching his every move.

I keep my eyes closed to survey movement behind the darkened doorways — figures standing comatose under the silent influence of a pirate king.

"A lesson in salvation," Taeia replies, glancing at the battle line as he approaches. "I could have killed you last time but I left you to the elements."

"The Kelph elite you've just obliterated, you mean."

"The same thing: elements under my control."

"Like the people in a trance behind those doorways?"

This brings a callous smile from my ex-comrade, followed by another look at the suspended slate and glass above us.

"If I whisper one word, everything above rains down on you."

"So, what are you waiting for?"

"You and your girl guides to leave before it's too late,"

"We're here to rescue you," Eaiwin states, bringing a loud laugh from our nemesis.

"*Rescue me* when you can barely defend yourself. I'll make the offer one more time: *leave before it's too late.*"

"Not without you," I reply, watching as my fire-red Williynx regains its strength.

"Once again, you make the wrong choice, Guppy Grayling, only this time your friends are going to pay the price."

A stamp of Taeia's foot causes the ice floor to crack ... a spider web of cracks spreading towards the doorways as I realise the trap that's been set. The trap's not for me but for two friends who float through the doorway: Lucy and Noah.

They're suspended in a trance, surrounded by Blood-seekers who hover in a similar comatose state, until Taeia stamps his foot again and the vampire army attack. I react in seconds, sending a flood of water towards the Bloodseekers, but my counter attack is thwarted by Taeia who looks on emotionlessly, holding out both hands with his eyes closed: a messiah leading evil disciples.

Lucy and Noah are sleepwalking to their death, no liquid gold armour to protect their bloodied bodies. It's a desperate sight I can't influence as another wave of water is absorbed by Taeia's cloak: the magical garment giving him new powers.

As blood drips onto the floor of ice, the mottleflies come to the rescue temporarily, whipping their black tails around the neck of the vampire army and yanking them away from their prey. This is followed by something more surprising ... mottlefly tails appearing through the cracked ice.

Hundreds of them whip towards Taeia's face, disappearing and re-appearing to avoid being absorbed by his magical cloak — a cloak unable to control one thing: the will of the winds.

It's the wind that spins Taeia off his feet ... a sudden gust of fury delivered by angry sky gods. It's the only way to explain how it overwhelms our lost boy, caught between a tornado of wind and twisting thunder — elements no longer under his control as black tails lash at his face, targeting hie eyes above all else.

It's only a brief respite as more enemies burst through the doorways, adding their own venom to proceedings, but a tornado of light meets them, sending them smashing into the tower walls. With Taeia caught in the crossfire, using his cloak to protect his damaged eyes, a pathway of glittering stars floods through the shattered windows: a sign a rescue might still be possible.

Reinforcements appear through the ice floor, the welcome sight of warrior women entering battle, covering their mouths as the oxygen drains out the atmosphere. We've got seconds to save Lucy and Noah.

"Move!" Mylisia orders — the queen who leads this rescue mission — her long hair turning into daggers as they shoot towards the charm hypnotising Lucy and Noah, giving me a chance to drag Lucy and Noah within a Velinis charm: bubbles of protection the Bloodseekers attack seconds later.

"The sky channel!" Mylisia shouts, pushing me towards the portal of stars the mottleflies fill, the entrance guarded by my loyal Williynx. "Now!"

Gasping for breath, I fire out a final blast of steel bullets as I spin towards the shattered windows, hoping our protective barriers are enough to get us to safety. No Jacqus appear this time, leaving critical cover to warrior queens who seem less affected by the lack of oxygen — the final touch of sorcery from an apprentice king who vanishes out of sight seconds later.

With Lucy and Noah surrounded by protective light, I use the Magneia charm to guide them to the sky channel, leaving the Zordeya army to deal with the remaining threat. The whipping wind eases as we enter the portal of stars, stretching in a diagonal line towards an unknown destination.

For the sake of my friends, I hope it's Zilom or The Royisin Heights. Mylisia waves me on, containing an enemy with her blades of hair and blinding gold dust — the look on her face suggesting Lucy and Noah might have run out of time.

18

END GAME

With blood streaking through the sky, The Royisin Heights bursts into life — reclusive witches and wizards blasting out of their reclusive dwellings, rushing to Lucy and Noah's aid.

Flying through the sky channel linking two worlds, Lucy and Noah float lifelessly as more Bloodseekers appear, clashing with a Society cavalry who swarm into the portal of stars.

Farraday appears with Kaira, whipping out Promesiun charms that send the vampire army scattering, but only momentarily as a flood of Axyiam join the fray ... hundreds of them surging into battle on pathways of fire ... joined by a vast reptilian crew who spit their venom.

Farraday isn't conditioned for war anymore, saying so himself recently, but the sight of Lucy and Noah under attack has triggered his warrior instinct, trying to create a distraction as the Zordeya army blast into sight, targeting the vampire army.

With one brutal act, the warrior women snap the Bloodseekers' necks with hair morphing into chains ... chains that tighten and pull with a sudden force.

War rages in the skies and Taeia Renn is nowhere to be seen — another sign of a coward at large. The last war had a 'no children die' code, seemingly still in place as familiar faces enter the fray. They might have arrived too late, though, as blood drips from Lucy and Noah's bodies.

This isn't their war, I think, remembering how uncomfortable they were at the thought of battle, although this helps little in a chamber of death. Getting them *out of here* is the primary aim, leading me to call Conrad into action, but he's got problems of his own.

With every member of our collective army engaged with an enemy, it rests on me to get Lucy and Noah to safety. Using the Infernisi charm to wrap myself in rings of fire, I activate my liquid-gold armour as additional protection, making sure material magic is in play at all times.

One mistake and I'm dead, dodging through blasts of enemy fire — bullet rain, twisting thunder, swords of lightning and cursed venom — desperate to reach Lucy and Noah before it's too late.

Farraday gets there first, lifting their lifeless bodies onto my Williynx.

"Take them home," he says, looking too weak for another battle, but a Society soldier is a soldier until the end.. "To The Cendryll where help is on hand."

"They're dead," I whisper, fighting back tears as our co-ordinated army contains the enemy.

"They're alive and in desperate need of help, so *take them back now* before it's too late."

"Come on, Guppy," Conrad urges, appearing alongside me. "*Now.*"

It's enough to get us moving, darting through the battlefield and through a sky portal, courtesy of our feathered friends familiar with the secrets of the skies. The Cendryll skylight comes into view, its beam of light stretching towards us.

The light is another form of protection, I imagine, shielding us against any surprises as we make our way to safety. The skylight turns to liquid at the touch of Williynx feathers: the very magic we'll need to save two battle-ravaged friends.

As the sky bleeds, we enter through the skylight onto the S.P.M.A. logo decorating the ground floor. Lucy and Noah's broken bodies are placed alongside one another as Casper and Philomeena clap the faculty into action, doors lining the ground floor swinging open as every available witch and wizard goes to work, trying to help our friends cheat death.

"We need mottleflies," I say, turning to Casper who offers no reply. "Where are they with their life-saving balm?"

I also want to ask where the hell he's been — the great Society legend who stands back when *his own daughter* is swarmed by the enemy. The petulant side of me subsides when I study the scars covering his hands, arms and neck: a man who's done more than enough for our magical world.

He never wanted any of us to return to battle, happier when Kaira was travelling in peaceful realms. It was our choice in the end, something I need to remember each time I stare death in the face.

"We're not in the sky realms, Guppy," Casper replies as he rolls up his sleeves. "It's Society magic or nothing."

"Well, *come on then*!" I shout at the crowd forming around us. "*Liqin!*"

A touch on the shoulder from Casper calms my anger.

"Easy, Guppy. Emotions do little in critical situations, as you well know, so control them if you want to save your friends."

I kneel beside Lucy and Noah as Casper takes charge, studying the Quij who hover nearby, ready to enact the funeral ritual I desperately want to be stopped.

"Quintz to stop the bleeding," Philomeena instructs to the onlookers, "then Srynx Serum and Williynx feathers to draw the venom out."

"Will it work?" Conrad asks as Jacob appears, going pale at the sight of slow death.

"It might, Conrad. It just might."

"Keep your penchants on them," Kaira's aunt adds. "Every touch of Society magic matters now."

Jacob joins us, kneeling alongside me as he places his penchant ring on Noah's chest where the deepest wound is, bubbling with venom. My brother doesn't flinch as the venom soaks his hand, covering it in a green stain.

"Jacob," I mutter but I know he's not moving now.

"We can save them," he replies, keeping his eyes fixed on Lucy and Noah. "We just have to draw some of the venom out."

"Casper didn't say anything about that," Conrad comments, his penchant ring on Noah's broken ankles — mine resting on Lucy's neck.

"No, he didn't but Philomeena did," Jacob replies. "'Every touch of Society magic matters.' They were the words she used — the reason our penchants are so important. See how their penchant stones are discolouring?"

"Destroying their chances of carrying on in the S.P.M.A. if they survive," Conrad adds.

"Right," Jacob says, "so we need to drain the venom from them before the Quintz remedy kicks in. I doubt they'll thank us if they wake up in above-ground houses, knowing they can never come back here. Memories wiped as thanks for protecting our world."

"Okay," I say, watching as a similar green stain covers my right hand. My penchant stones maintain their topaz-blue glow: a sign Society sorcery is holding up against the venom marking us all.

Another clap from Casper causes Lucy and Noah's bodies to rise, but not in the way Smyck's did during his death ritual. Our friends aren't dead yet, signalled by the Quij keeping a respectful distance. Instead, a group of Society elders form a line beneath Lucy and Noah's bodies — each of them holding a vial of Quintz remedy, used to stop bleeding.

With the vials opened, the white remedy stretches upwards, covering the wounds on Lucy and Noah's bodies. As it sinks into the wounds, our friends exhale softly: a sign there's fight in them yet. The Fateful Eight appear through a swinging door seconds later, ushered away quickly by Farraday.

Scribberals have rattled in their bedrooms, no doubt, the message triggering a desire to see battle playing out in real time. It's a reminder of how quickly life can change — eight young witches and wizards struggling to make the grade.

The sight of Lucy and Noah's blood-soaked bodies might have given them second thoughts, although I doubt it from the nature of their characters. They're all *desperate* to belong here; a decision in the hands of Jacob when the time comes.

As the group of ageing wizards continue to administer the Quintz remedy, the Williynx lower their heads, releasing coloured feathers over Lucy and Noah until our friends are completely covered. Unlike the death ritual formed by the Quij, this is our version of mottlefly magic: a remedy to dance with death until life is restored.

Kaira appears through the skylight a few minutes later, accompanied by Farraday who's survived battle thankfully. She joins us as Lucy and Noah remain still. The image brings back the memory of Smyck rotating in this very place, wrapped in a cocoon of colour as the Cendryll masses looked on — arms raised in a death ritual I've come to know well.

I let the tears fall as my friends bodies remain motionless, suggesting the potion isn't penetrating the venom.

"It's too late," I whisper as Conrad puts an arm around my shoulders. "We got to them too late."

"There's still time, Guppy," Philomeena replies — the maternal figure who's saved me in so many ways. "Bloodseekers' venom isn't so different to Society creatures; we just need to find the right fusion of magic to rid Lucy and Noah of it."

"Taeia's responsible for this," I mutter as Lucy and Noah's bodies return to the marble floor, "and I'm going to kill him when we find him."

"You can't kill a Winter King, Guppy," Kaira states, kneeling to study Society magic at work.

"I can do my best and he isn't a Winter King yet."

"Kaira's right," Jacob comments. "Any attempt to kill him will spark a war between worlds."

"So he's won?"

"He's winning but fading," Farraday adds, releasing Spintz charms above the ritual. "The reason he retreated when battle raged."

"Fading? How is he fading when he just drained the atmosphere of oxygen?"

"He *almost* drained the sky of oxygen until an army swarmed him, including mottleflies who targeted his eyes with their tails: not a coincidence."

"You think the mottleflies have nudged Taeia onto the right path?" I ask, sensing where Farraday's going with this.

"Maybe. His eyesight's damaged now and all Winter King's gain the gift of blind sight."

"When they've completed a seven-year pilgrimage, proving themselves worthy."

"Which he's one step closer to," Kaira adds, echoing Farraday's comments, "once he realises he's more powerful with limited vision."

"How do we know he's going to be more powerful?"

"We don't," Kaira replies, "but if his weakness becomes his greatest strength it might be the turning point he needs, *finally* realising his true home is on the throne of Devreack."

"Proof his destiny can't be avoided."

"He's avoided his destiny pretty well so far," I counter, "sparking war along the way."

"All kings spark war, Guppy," Casper interjects, "but Taeia hasn't directly harmed anyone, suggesting he's still at war with himself. When the vision we've all seen plays out — with Taeia charging towards Devreack — the battle between kings begins ... when time stops and dead legends return. For now, we have lives to save and wounds to heal."

It's a point I can't argue with as crowds appear on the balconies of each floor, watching a dance with death. The longer this war goes on, the more I struggle with the idea of continuing the mission.

We've abandoned Night Ranging to protect a neighbouring realm, encountering death and destruction on the way. Now, we're supposed to continue on that path with two of our own clinging on to life.

I've accepted my role in the Society but feel my old impulsive self returning, which isn't good news for Taeia.

Winter Kings can't be killed, but what world stands back when a king in waiting becomes a curse?

Heir apparent he might be, but until he takes the throne he's a pretender in my eyes: a pretender who needs to accept his destiny or perish fighting against it. I don't mind either way although I am certain of one thing: the next time we meet I'll be ready.

19

SAD TONES

The evening passes slowly as emergency procedures continue, Lucy and Noah's bodies remaining lifeless as a magical fusion seeps through them. I sit alongside the others, our hands remaining in place on our friends' wounds, secretly praying they make it.

Whoever we're praying to isn't offering an answer at the moment — the sight of the Quij forming a circle of light not a good sign. Casper, Philomeena and Farraday maintain a protective wall around us, using the Infernisi charm to ensure other members keep a respectful distance.

The rings of fire are an unusual sight in a faculty of unified witches and wizards, but a sense of tragedy always draws a crowd. With concerned faces remaining on the balconies and spiral staircase, the dance of death continues.

Williynx feathers have always come to our rescue until now, but we're fighting an alien curse from a distant realm this time, the reason the feathers don't jolt Lucy and Noah to life. Remedies continue to pour onto the S.P.M.A. logo, multi-coloured strands of light forming over their bodies.

It's as close to a death ritual as you can get although I tell myself otherwise, ignoring my minor injuries to offer what I can: a touch of magic from my penchant stones. Conrad, Kaira and Jacob do the same, kneeling alongside me in silent unity, waiting for Society sorcery to come to the rescue but it doesn't.

"What else can we do?" I ask Casper who stands within our protective circles of fire.

"Wait, Guppy; that's all we can do."

"But it's *not working*."

"The night will tell us that. This is no simple curse; it's venom from a realm beyond our normal powers."

"So, we're guessing?" Jacob comments, turning to look at Farraday who offers a grim smile.

"We're *adapting*," Farraday replies. "The very thing you're teaching your students. War isn't a fairytale, Jacob, even in a magical universe able to bend time and space. We're in a battle with death now, doing all we can to save our brave comrades."

"They should have stayed as Night Rangers," I mutter, feeling another wave of grief forming. "It was too soon for them."

"It was too soon for you," Philomeena replies, as stylish as ever in a silver-grey trouser suit. "The very reason magical laws dictated eighteen to be the age of entry. No one wants to see a child die."

That returns a silence to the proceedings until a glimmer of hope appears … as Lucy opens her eyes for a moment … then again … blinking tears of blood.

"Lucy," I whisper, keeping my right hand on her shattered ankles. "It's Guppy. Can you hear me?"

My friend nods, studying the blanket of Williynx

feathers covering her. "We made it out alive," she whispers as she tries to move, grimacing in pain as she does.

"Take it easy," Kaira suggests. "You're badly injured. The less you move, the better it will be."

Lucy nods, placing her head back on the marble floor — a Society glowing with light as the logo continues to glimmer like an operating table infused with a strange superpower. The tone of things change when she turns to look at Noah, more tears of blood running down her face at the sight of her boyfriend's brutal wounds.

She looks at us for signs of reassurance and we try our best to offer them, but the miracle of magic hasn't found a way to jolt Noah into life, leaving the minutes to tick by towards a conclusion I can't bear to think of.

———

MORE TIME PASSES AS LUCY FLICKERS IN AND OUT OF consciousness, her eyes fluttering as if she's reliving the recent battle. The only signs of life from Noah are the regular, slow pulse in his neck: a glimmer of hope.

Hope fades, though, as midnight draws close known as the witching hour to some — this Fire Witch feeling powerless as Lucy coughs up blood and Noah remains still ... the beginning of the end.

A sigh of relief falls over The Cendryll as Lucy opens her eyes again, this time able to sit up, lifting her right hand to signal survival. Under normal circumstances, a cry of joy would ring around the magical faculty but Noah's showing no similar sign of recovery.

The bands of multi-coloured light fade on his body as the swinging doors come to a standstill, followed by the Quij fluttering closer to him, releasing threads of light to begin a ritual of death: the sign our friend has lost his battle for survival.

———

WE STAY UP ALL NIGHT WITH LUCY, SITTING ON THE MARBLE floor after Noah's body has been taken to the tunnels, ready for his final journey to Gilweean — the resting place of the dead. Tears of blood continue to run down her face, the consequences of a curse seeping out of her. She sits silently for hours, watching Noah's passage to Gilweean on a Pano-rilum, the floating piece of parchment giving her some sense of solace.

"I don't know what happened," she finally says, watching as the small, wooden boat carrying Noah passes through a glimmering waterfall, entering the peaceful realm of Gilweean. "One minute I'm with Sylvian Creswell and the next I start to sink, struggling for air as something swarms around me."

"Taeia's work," Jacob says, using the Canvia charm to draw random images in the air. "Killer or not, he's got blood on his hands now."

"I don't know if Sylvian made it," Lucy adds, unable to mention Noah's name.

We share a glance between each other, none of us able to confirm this either way.

"And Aarav?" Lucy prompts, wondering if Noah's uncle got caught in Taeia's hypnotic trap.

"Hunting Taeia down by the looks of things," Conrad replies, pointing to the mystical wizard shimmering in and out of sight on the floating parchment, gliding above the connected sky towers where his nephew fell victim to a former comrade's powers.

"He shouldn't be out there on his own," Kaira states, sitting cross legged alongside me.

"He isn't," I reply, standing to point at the swarm of dots surrounding him. "Sky urchins ready to go to war again."

With the sight of Noah floating to the bottom of the Gilweean ocean, his cocooned body spinning above a carpet of shimmering colour, Lucy turns away from the Panorilum, unable to stomach the visions of shattered towers and bridges: a reminder of what's been lost.

"You should try to get some sleep," I suggest, checking on the state of her ankles which are still badly bruised. The wounds on her chest don't look much better.

"The nightmares start as soon as I close my eyes," she replies before adding, "I wish I could have said goodbye."

There's nothing to say to this — nothing that will help at least — so I join my brother, creating random designs with my finger, beginning with a rabbit that hops across Jacob's field of flowers. Kaira adds trees in full blossom before Conrad joins in, creating a sky full of kites.

It's a peaceful vision, filling The Cendryll with a light show of a different kind — one free of visions of death. That's until Lucy steps beside me, adding a gravestone near the furthest tree ... blossom falling over the name she adds in simple handwriting: Noah Khan. Turning our creative focus on the gravestone, we add flowers around the grave, helping Lucy to say goodbye.

———

WITH LUCY RECOVERING ON THE FOURTH FLOOR AND KAIRA above ground with her dad and aunt, I spend the early morning with Jacob who's preparing for another day of teaching. Conrad's still asleep, giving me some rare alone time with my brother.

We discuss Lucy's condition, thankful the tears of blood have dried up, before returning to the inevitable topic of Taeia Renn — still at large in a crumbling prison of his own making.

"I didn't use the Exhibius charm to call the Jacqus," I say as Jacob sips a cup of Liqin, a morning tradition he has now. "When they saved me from the Kelph elite, I mean. Sianna said we had to use the Exhibius charm to call them, but I didn't have time."

"Casper called the Jacqus," Jacob replies, sitting at the dining table in my fourth-floor quarters. "He's been monitoring things closely."

"He's not going to make an appearance, then?"

"From the wings, like he said. Casper's played his part, Guppy. We all know that. He's a soldier at heart but he's not the man he was."

"I know. It's just something I need to get my head around. He's always been there, leading the way in times of crisis."

"He still is but in a different way now. He helped to restore peace here, struggling with his scars in his own way. His focus is Kaira now, doing everything he can to keep her safe wherever she travels."

"And what about you? Do you think you'll stick to teaching from now on?"

"I think I need a holiday," Jacob replies, brushing his long, dark hair away from his eyes. "Teenage witches and wizards are hard work."

"Well, you managed to knock me into shape."

"After almost getting us killed a few times."

"I was testing you."

Jacob gives me a familiar smile — the brother who's stepped back from battle, returning to a different line of duty.

"Just come back alive," he adds, holding my gaze as he sips his Liqin. "There's not much life without love, is there?"

"I'll be fine, Jacob."

"You always say that."

"It's almost over, anyway. Taeia's running out of places to hide."

"Which makes him more desperate," my brother replies. "The reason Casper's taken Kaira above ground, I think, preparing her for what happens next. Noah's death has rocked the Society, Guppy. Children should never be victims of war."

I rub my penchant bracelet, remembering how Noah struggled with the idea of battle, eventually committing to the cause. Now, I have to struggle with the image of a friend sinking to the bottom of an ocean lined with dead legends.

"I'll be careful," I promise, taking a sip from Jacob's cup. "And I've got a growing army around me."

Uttering 'Comeuppance', Jacob takes out his Follygrin. Opening the circular, leather-bound artefact, he rubs his finger over the letter 'A'. Waiting for the letter to bleed into the familiar words *Ask and you will Find*, he says, "Casper Renn".

The pages flick to the letter 'C' and I lean closer, studying the moving illustration of Casper, Philomeena and Kaira walking through Founders' Quad: the family trio spending some time away from all things magical.

"Something tells me Casper's going to be spending more time above ground," Jacob comments, rotating the bevelled edge of the Follygrin to zoom in. "He's been going back to 12 Spyndall Street more often, talking things through with

Philomeena. Kaira's chosen her own path, meaning they can only protect her from a distance now."

"The Cendryll wouldn't be the same without them."

"Everything moves on in the end, Guppy, including the people we love the most."

Which makes me think of Kaira and Noah again: one friend gone and another preparing to step back from Society duty again. Loss is becoming a familiar visitor, arriving in recurring waves that leave their mark.

Thoughts of love and loss make me reminisce, thinking about the first time I met Kaira. I smile at the memory of our first trip above-ground together, me babbling on as Kaira started to glaze over, a trip to Merrymopes giving her a welcome time out: magical milkshakes to make everything better.

I watch my friend walk into Wimples sweet shop, wondering what an above-ground life would have been like — easy living for the uninitiated. It's a thought that passes seconds after it's formed, magic always trumping monotony even when danger takes centre stage.

"Keep an eye on Lucy when I'm gone," I say to my brother who gets up from the dining table, preparing for another day with The Fateful Eight.

"She loved Noah," I comment, remembering how it took ages for them to get together — Noah pining after Zoe Tallis before realising he was confusing love with desire. They weren't an obvious couple but they worked, becoming more at one with each other over time. War ripped that away from them, leading me to reevaluate my own role in the Society.

Do I want to be fighting forever? A Fire Witch on perma-nent duty? The idea of a peaceful life appeals to me too, mixing new charms in the safety of The Cendryll. Family's never far from my thoughts either, wondering if I'll ever have kids of my own.

If I did have children, would I want them fighting to protect the S.P.M.A.? I'd definitely fight against it just like Casper and Philomeena did when Kaira edged closer to the battlefield. It was the reason they brought Kaira into the Society in the first place, sensing the increasing danger above ground.

Things took a turn for the worse and a young crew was thrust into battle; a battle we survived thankfully, putting us on different paths until the stars revealed their secrets, unleashing hidden powers in a bitter boy with vengeance in his soul.

As Jacob heads off to meet his students, I think about Noah again: a gentle soul with a wicked sense of humour. Thinking about death makes you vulnerable in war, though, introducing an element of doubt that slows your reflexes.

A knock on the door draws me away from thoughts of death, turning to see Lucy peering in the room.

"Can I come in?" she asks, her pixie face pale with grief.

"Of course, Lucy."

She joins me at the dining table, asking if I've got anything to drink. Not knowing if she means tea or something stronger, I decided to fill the Parasil with Srynx Serum: a remedy to heal wounds.

"How are you feeling?" I ask, turning the brass tap on the glass contraption.

"Sore," Lucy replies with a sad smile. She sips the orange liquid, her bruised hands and arms shaking a little. "I never thought I'd be here," she adds, blowing on the hot remedy.

"I don't know what to say."

"There's nothing to say, Guppy. We fought, we got captured and Noah's dead."

Her bluntness shocks me as does the bruising covering her body.

"Taeia won't win, Lucy," I state, holding onto the principles we're fighting for: peace and preservation. "No matter what he does, he can't stop destiny."

"He's still got plenty of support. It's how he ambushed me so quickly, and if he *does* become king he'll have even more power."

"Pure power at least; the only power a Winter King can possess."

"Along with a taste for blood."

"Blood that strengthens but doesn't distort."

"I don't think he deserves to be saved now," Lucy states, keeping her eyes lowered as the Srynx Serum eases the shaking in her hands and arms.

"I agree," I reply, "but leaving him to his own devices makes things worse for us."

"Because he's one of ours," Lucy adds, "or was."

"Meaning if we don't lend a helping hand, we've left the sky realms vulnerable to a Society wizard. You don't have to think too hard to see where that leads."

"Another war between worlds."

"Right, so we have to carry on until Taeia submits or implodes."

"What do you think he'll do?" Lucy asks, holding my gaze.

"I honestly don't know, but it's going to get worse before it gets better," I reply, wondering how the story of a boy storming a fortress will end.

Suicide, submission and obliteration are all possibilities as a royal throne spins, about to bring dead kings to life — ready to lock their target into position.

20

A QUESTION OF REDEMPTION

After Lucy heads off to another rehabilitation session, I tidy my fourth-floor quarters to keep my mind off Noah. It doesn't really work, but until Conrad wakes up I haven't got much else to do. Liqin's eased Conrad into a deep sleep, the remedy used to shake off hallucinations.

He's struggling with weird dreams more than hallucinations ... of Noah being ravaged by Bloodseekers as Taeia looks on. It's a vision that's made Conrad *very angry*, saying he's going to kill Taeia before he gets a chance to become a king. As much as I've tried to talk him out of this, Conrad simply isn't listening. Fate has one thing in store for Taeia, he says, and he's got another.

His anger's fuelled by grief and guilt, punishing himself for not being there to help Noah, made worse by the fact he had to watch his friend die. I doubt he's *actually* going to try to kill Taeia, but it's still a genuine concern and one I'll have to raise with Casper if he continues to pursue this thought.

Like I said to Lucy, doing anything to anger the sky gods will backfire *massively* on the S.P.M.A. — the last thing we need in the current climate. We need to stick to the plan, doing whatever it takes to get Taeia to divert his course. There are hopeful signs, at least, including his faltering smile and damaged eyesight.

The whipping wind turned against him, rendering him helpless as the mottleflies' tails ravaged his face. His cloak did little to thwart the attack, hanging in the air until we got Lucy and Noah out of there. Once again, the sky gods proved who's really in control up there — not an apprentice king but a timeless magic that's infinite in scope: more proof that a Winter King answers to forces greater than himself.

Noah's paid the ultimate price for Taeia's reckless choices: a life extinguished by cursed blood. Another wave of grief forms at the thought of this, the dining table wiped clean for the third time — anything to help keep my mind off visions of death. At the sound of movement from the bedroom, I make some toast and tea, wanting the comfort of normality for a while.

When Scriberrals start rattling throughout The Cendryll, I'll know it's time to return to the sky realms, but for now I want to enjoy a bit of peace and quiet with the boy I love, struggling to shake off a sense of guilt. Conrad appears from the bedroom fifteen minutes later, showered and dressed in unironed blue jeans and a grey T-shirt.

"How did you sleep?" I ask, careful not to mention Noah's name.

"Not great," he replies, glancing at the toast I've put on the table.

He rubs at the scar on his neck, a sign he's still struggling with his anger. "I just want this over with now so we can get on with our lives here."

"So do I?"

"And I'm obviously not going to try and kill Taeia, as much as I want to."

"It would spark war between us."

"I *know*, Guppy," he snaps, his face reddening as he does. "He just doesn't deserve to live, but there's nothing I can do about that."

Placing the teapot on the table, I sit opposite my Conrad, annoyed he's taking his anger out on me. It's not the time for a lover's tiff so I let it pass, pouring some tea for him.

"Lucy came by early for a chat," I say, sipping the tea.

Conrad reaches for some toast, blinking as he does. The visions of Noah's death haven't left him yet, meaning he'll need more Liqin soon. "How is she?"

"Bruised and shellshocked."

"It shouldn't have happened," Conrad comments, biting the piece of toast. "We should have been there."

"I *was* there, remember?"

This brings a pause between us, our relationship about to be tested in a new way. "I meant ..."

"Meant what?" I snap. "That an army of women weren't good enough?"

"I didn't say that, Guppy."

"Then what *are* you saying because it seems like I'm getting the brunt of your anger."

"I feel *guilty,* Guppy."

"Of course you do. Noah was your best friend but *nothing* could save him, Guppy, not even ancient Society magic."

"The coward couldn't even do his own dirty work, trapping him in a swarm of Bloodseekers before vanishing when he got hurt, and he calls himself a king."

"Well, if Farraday's right, the mottleflies have nudged him onto the right path by partially blinding him. Obviously, only Devreack can offer the gift of blind sight, but if

Taeia can *see more* ... see *deeper* within himself ... the mottle-flies' attack might be the turning point we need."

"Let's hope so," Conrad replies, looking lost in a way I haven't seen for a long time.

It's as if he's regressing to a younger version of himself — the lost boy I first met in The Cendryll — sullen and quiet after the sudden death of his mum. His dad died a few months later: one of the sacrificial seven giving their lives to extinguish a critical threat. Loss weighs heavier on Conrad than most, something I need to remember in times like this.

"He'll always be with us," I offer, holding Conrad's hand across the table. "He might rest in the waters of Gilweean, but we'll always be able to pay our respects."

"The Hallowed Lawn," Conrad mutters, offering a pained smile as he does. "The place where dead legends rise from the ashes."

"Right, and Noah's a legend now."

Conrad stands, buoyed by the thought of this. "He would have loved that," he says, "knowing he'd be talked about forever."

"Who wouldn't?" I prompt, wanting to hold him.

He seems to have the same thought, standing to meet me at the end of the table.

"It will be nice to pay Noah a visit when this is over. We could play a game of Rucklz."

"I'm not sure ghosts can play Rucklz," I add, hugging him tightly.

"We can give it a try. Maybe get The Fateful Eight involved."

"And scare them to death?"

A laugh fills the room — a slow release of grief that lessens the tension in Conrad's body. "Noah would love that."

I kiss his forehead, running a hand through his copper-blonde hair. He's strangely vulnerable, resting his head on my shoulders: a loving moment we both need.

"We'll be called back up there soon," he says, closing his eyes as I kiss his forehead again. "The ones that are going back, that is."

"Lucy needs time to heal and Jacob's resettled into teaching."

"Leaving the three of us: you, me and Kaira."

"Assuming Kaira returns with us. She's above ground with her dad and aunt again: a sign she might be having second thoughts."

"She'll return with us," Conrad states, pulling me closer. "Kaira just likes to keep her distance now."

It's a reality I haven't fully absorbed, the realisation my best friend has moved on. She's returned to the battlefield for her own reasons — reasons being discussed with her dad and aunt now.

"I just hope we get out of this alive."

"We will," Conrad replies, returning the kiss. "We'll be back to our morning flights before you know it, gliding through The Winter Quarter."

"We should invite Lucy on them," I suggest. "It might help her to heal. We could go to all the places the four of us ventured to: a pilgrimage of our own."

"Lucy would like that, I think."

"I suppose it's just a case of waiting now," I add, "until we're called back."

"To watch a battle between kings: dead and alive," Conrad comments.

As The Cendryll moves to slower rhythms, reflecting the weight of loss carried by all, I feel drawn to the skylight again, wondering if we'll get any clues to how this all ends.

A Winter King can only be killed by time, meaning time's about to manoeuvre Taeia onto his true path or obliterate him out of existence.

With Noah dead, I should favour the second option, but I hold on to the words of a Society legend who's sacrificed more than most: Casper Renn. No doubt, he's reminding Kaira of the mercy mission we're on even now — the way of a man conditioned to honour Society principles.

With Noah dead, mercy isn't a word on anyone's tongue, but something tells me the compass hasn't shifted away from compassion: the compassion offered to a girl abandoned by a power-hungry mother, and extended to Conrad when his world fell apart.

It's the compassion Casper's consistently shown to wayward witches and wizards, including my mum. If anyone senses how this is going to end, it's Casper Renn: another wizard burdened with greatness from a young age. Maybe he understands Taeia's rage, being skilled at containing his own.

After all, how would it feel to find out your life was predetermined? The realisation that free will wasn't a luxury you had? How many Winter Kings have fought their fate? How many have survived to tell the tale? Questions only the shifting stars have answers to, waiting to call on us again when Taeia Renn storms an abandoned kingdom.

TEASER CHAPTER BOOK 5

Preparation time becomes slow time as things return to normal in The Cendryll. With Lucy recovering under the watchful eye of Philomeena, Kaira continues her above-ground walks with her dad, moving between magical and non-magical living. Jacob thinks Casper's going to spend more time above ground soon, holed up in 12 Spyndall Street unburdened by magical mysteries.

12 Spyndall Street is Kaira's old home — original home even — before the wonders of the S.P.M.A. took hold. It's

the wonder I want to get back to, hoping the final battle to save Taeia from certain doom is a swift one. It almost certainly won't be but wishful thinking comes in handy when you're dealing with grief.

Everything feels a little *flat* without Noah around ... his gentle spirit and comic timing carrying us along on our adventures. He's gone now, though, resting at the bottom of the Gilweean ocean: the first child casualty of war. It sounds brutal when you put it that way, but there's no easy way of putting it.

Bloodseekers killed him with their venom under the silent influence of Taeia Renn, not something Noah's uncle — Aarav Khan — is going to let rest. Aarav's already blazing through the skies on the hunt for Taeia, all notions of a mercy mission discarded as he seeks vengeance.

Part of me wonders if Kaira's morning walks with her dad are part of the bigger plot, possibly to stop Aarav trying to kill Taeia, something that will send shock waves through both magical worlds. Time dictates a Winter King's beginning and end, and time answers to no witch or wizard — something Aarav understands — but understanding and acceptance are two different things.

I've been doing some wandering of my own, hiding out in The Glass Arch with Conrad as I come to terms with my own grief. We've tried to spend time with Lucy but it hasn't helped, her mental scars being deeper than her physical ones. In the end, Philomeena suggested we visit Lucy in the evenings when she's more alert, probably due to healing properties of Srynx Serum.

No magical potion removes feelings, though, so grief has to be negotiated in the normal way. Losing a friend is one thing, but losing a boyfriend is something else altogether. It's a thought that makes me wonder what I'll do if Conrad dies in the last battle? The boy who's healed more than he knows. Conrad refuses to discuss the topic of death — a flicker of anger crossing his face when I do.

Noah was his best friend and he still feels guilty, believing he should have been there to protect him, but he *couldn't* be because we were all navigating our own paths: a simple way of weakening our collective power. In the end, it's not our war but a battle to protect a sacred throne from the very person who should be occupying it: the mercy mission we agreed to in the beginning.

With Jacob returning to his teaching duties, Conrad and I enjoy the peace of The Glass Arch — the training chamber I learnt my craft in with Kaira and Jacob. It has its own associations of grief, the memory of Smyck guiding me resonating now, as well as the memory of how he died protecting Kaira. There's no escaping loss now wherever we go.

It's present in The Cendryll with Lucy's recovery, in The Glass Arch and in the sky realms that continue to occupy my mind. Friends, comrades and Winter Kings have died in a short period of time, and it's likely more will, but a Society soldier has an immovable duty to protect what's sacred — the sacred element being a spinning throne ready to awaken dead kings.

"Do you remember Jacob talking about travelling?" Conrad says as we activate a flight charm, lifting us towards the glass roof. "When the last war came to an end."

I nod, studying the daisy wrapped around my wrist, spinning like a propeller as we rise higher. "Getting away from all this for a while," I add, wondering about all the places Kaira's been to recently. "It would be fun."

"A break from the madness," Conrad comments with a

smile, adjusting the path of his flight to move closer to me, taking my left hand as he does.

We hug as we rise slowly, happy to be in no hurry as The Glass Arch filters the light flooding in, the vast chamber a perfect place to recuperate from the fallout of battle. Something about the interior of the space brings back sad memories, so we spend the mornings forming a different ritual, floating through the glass ceiling to the peaceful space beyond.

Unlike The Cendryll's skylight, the steel-and-glass structure doesn't look out over any part of the S.P.M.A. Instead, a blanket of soft light fills the space, offering the peace and tranquillity we both need. Perched at the pinnacle of the enormous arch, Conrad and I hold hands, sitting in silence for a while as the soft light washes over us, helping to steady the shifting visions of death we're both struggling with.

"I wonder where we'd go if we flew off from here," Conrad adds, dressed in jeans and a black T-shirt.

"Probably to a part of Society Square," I reply, swinging my legs at the top of our platform in the sky.

"We could pay Jalem, Harvey and Ilina (check) a visit."

"They'd want to talk about Noah," I say, knowing how Conrad would react to that. "Maybe after we finish the business in the sky realms."

"Putting our lives on the line again."

"Are you having doubts?"

Conrad shrugs, looking ahead as if he's hoping to spot something in the flood of light. "I'd never go against the Society, but then I'm not going to lie and say it's going to be easy."

"To save Taeia, you mean?"

"To *try* to save him, at least, assuming Aarav doesn't get to him first."

"Aarav's to conditioned in war to go against Society rules."

"He's lost his nephew to a killer-king."

I decide not to reply, knowing there's no point in stating that Taeia didn't kill Noah. As far as Conrad is concerned, Taeia's guilty and that's all there is to it, making me wonder what he *is* going to do when they come face-to-face again. I've had dreams of how this all ends ... the sky realms in flames in some ... under the sinister control of black Williynx in others ... and Taeia swarmed by dead kings in others.

No dream has a happy ending which could mean something or nothing. In the end, the only reliable vision is Thylas Renn's ... of Taeia storming the white fortress of Devreack on a black Williynx. It's a vision witnessed by all the main players in this battle: the moment the winds of fate enter the stage for the final curtain call.

I've had more dreams of my own death recently, falling under a deluge of bullet rain as Taeia looks on ... thunder and lightning under his command as the skies submit to his silent influence. I always feel calm in these dreams although that changes when I wake up — dreams I haven't shared with anyone else.

"Let's do whatever we can to protect Devreack," I say, shifting the focus from Taeia as a killer king. "As long as that remains our focus, our boy-king's going to have a job penetrating our defences."

"He's done pretty well so far. Wasn't he surrounded by an entire army in the sky towers?"

I stop swinging my legs, containing my anger as I look at Conrad. "What does that mean?"

"It's just a question, Guppy."

"It sounds like an accusation. You know Taeia was

surrounded?"

"And he got away, proving how powerful he is."

"*And*?"

"And he's also retreated at every turn, eventually being overwhelmed by our combined forces."

"But we haven't been able to *stop him*, have we?"

"Maybe because he's The Winter King in waiting, and kings have unique powers. Are we *really* going over this again?"

"I just think we could be missing a critical point?" Conrad says.

"Which is?"

"That Thylas' vision completes itself with Taeia *destroying* the throne of Devreack; the reason why the vision is incomplete ... it's the end of the sky realms as we know them. We're working on the assumption that Taeia can't destroy the throne, but what if he's got *unique powers*? Powers Thylas' vision couldn't interpret. What if the darkness in him makes him stronger?"

"Then we've got a bigger battle on our hands, although I think you're overestimating Taeia's powers because of what happened to Noah. We can't avoid talking about it forever, Conrad. What happened to Noah could happen to us, something we *all* accepted before we stepped into this.

We honour Noah's memory by *winning* this war and re-establishing harmony in the sky realms, with *Taeia on the throne.* No other outcome restores the fragile allegiance up there."

"And if we can't?"

"We return to our duties here, doing whatever's necessary next. Our role ends when the war's won or lost, and then life goes on."

"When we can have a bit of fun."

"Why wait to have a bit of fun?"

"What have you got in mind?"

"A little parachute jump."

"Off here?" Conrad asks, a brightness returning to his eyes.

"Why not? The Glass Arch is a training chamber, after all. We normally smash the glass to learn how to control and reform it. Who's to say we can't use the glass in a different way?"

"To travel?"

I nod with a smile.

"But we're not in the sky realms, Guppy."

"We've ridden paths of ice created by the Williynx down here. Why would it be any different with glass fragments? All we need is momentum?"

"Are you sure?"

"Nope."

A reply which brings a well-needed laugh from my boy-wizard. "You're crazy, Guppy Grayling."

"Crazy enough to try it. Come on, let's create a ride we can show Lucy when she's feeling better. If it works, it can be a way of remembering Noah."

"And if it doesn't?"

"Someone can work out how to remember us."

With another laugh, Conrad nods his approval, letting go of my hand to prepare our experiment. As we activate the Velinis charm to create a bubble of protection around us, in preparation for the blizzard of glass about to explode around us, we whisper 'Promesiun', releasing a charge of coloured light onto the glimmering glass.

As The Glass Arch explodes into a thousand pieces, the Magneia charm is added to the sky dance, drawing the glass fragments towards us as we leap off the collapsing structure.

In two more moves, we have a pathway of glass stretching out under us and ropes of light in our hands, propelling us forwards.

It doesn't work straight away, the remaining shards of glass swirling around us to knock us off course, but we've done it enough times to know how to use material magic to fly through the sky: a simple matter of touch and timing. Our ropes of light add the momentum we need, and the Velinis charm protects us from the flying fragments.

We find our rhythm soon afterwards, riding the pathways of glass like skilled chariot riders, bending at the knees as we tilt one way then the other, gliding through the soft light in search of familiar surroundings. They appear soon after in the form of snow and an illuminated bridge below: the sign we're hovering over The Winter Quarter.

I'm not sure how the white light works here, sensing it takes you to the place occupying your thoughts. For obvious reasons, The Winter Quarter dominates our minds because it's the place linking the four of us. It's the realm Conrad and I used to fly over each morning, and the place where Noah realised where his heart belonged, his date with Zoe Tallis ending with him standing alone on The Sinking Bridge.

Lucy came to Noah's rescue then, offering the first touch of love that helped him see what he was missing. We can offer a loving touch of our own now, charting a new course that can act as a ritual between friends, marking love and loss in our own way.

"Noah would have loved this," Conrad says, offering a smile of thanks.

"And Lucy will too," I add, weaving on my pathway of glass as a familiar touch of colour comes into view: Williynx arriving at the ideal moment. "When she's ready."

"Thanks, Guppy."

"For what?"

"You know."

And I do ... a thanks for helping Conrad to stay afloat as grief takes hold again: an all-too familiar visitor for a boy who's lost so much.

"Come on," I say, wanting to enjoy this moment for as long as we can. "Let's reform The Glass Arch and get the Williynx to take us on."

This part doesn't need any further explanation, the two of us skilled in the use of the Repellia charm. With our feathered friends closing in, we return the glass fragments to their rightful place, watching as they move elegantly through the soft light. The shards of glass and steel reconnect and reform until the colossal arch can be seen through the light once more: a sign to jump onto our Williynx and continue our morning flight.

Thoughts of war remain but we do our best to ignore them, gliding through the snow that falls over The Winter Quarter, moving onto The Singing Quarter and beyond. We've got no particular destination in mind, happy to enjoy the peace of the morning until duty calls again.

Buy Book 5

ABOUT THE AUTHOR

I'm the author of the **Kaira Renn** series, **The Fire Witch Chronicles** and **Magic & Misdemeanours**, all set in The Society for the Preservation of Magical Artefacts. (S.P.M.A.)

If you enjoyed the book, please consider **leaving a review on Amazon.**

To receive updates and a chance to win free copies of future titles, sign up to my newsletter **here**.

You can also join my **Facebook group** dedicated the S.P.M.A. universe.

ALSO BY R.A. LINDO

THE S.P.M.A. UNIVERSE

5 books per series

Kaira Renn Series: origin series

The Fire Witch Chronicles: spin-off series one

Magic & Misdemeanours: spin-off series two

Printed in Great Britain
by Amazon

21260167R00119